M000166674

THE BILLIONAIRE'S OBSESSION
Kade

J. S. SCOTT

The Billionaire's Game

Copyright © 2014 by J. S. Scott

All rights reserved. No part of this document may be reproduced or transmitted in any form or by any means, electronic, mechanical, photocopying, recording, or otherwise, without prior written permission of the Author.

Edited by Faith Williams – The Atwater Group
Cover Design by Cali MacKay – Covers by Cali

ISBN: 978-1-939962-43-0 (Print)
ISBN: 978-1-939962-42-3 (E-Book)

Author Note

This book is dedicated to my two favorite people who have Telugu Indian blood: my dear friend, Rita, and my husband, Sri. Thank you for your help and for the insight into the Indian culture. Both of you are so extraordinary, and have been the wind beneath my wings when I needed your support. Thank you for answering my endless questions about Indian culture and history with so much patience.

Last year was an incredible year for me, and I'd like to thank all of my readers who continue to fall in love with my alpha billionaires. You are all so awesome and supportive. I'm grateful for every single one of you for helping my dreams come true!

Contents

Prologue

Southern California, Two Years Ago

The beaten, battered, and bruised woman lying on the living room floor of her apartment moaned weakly, barely conscious after the beating her husband had given her. She'd tried so hard to hide, to be in any room other than the one her husband had been in when he'd come home from work that day. Strangely, sadly, she was starting to know exactly when she was going to feel the pain of his wrath. Lately, it had been more and more often, usually for reasons she didn't exactly understand. She didn't talk back to him, she wasn't disobedient, and she got all of her household chores done. It didn't seem to matter. There was always some infraction, something that made her deserving of punishment.

Survive! Survive! Survive!

Opening one swollen eye, she stumbled painfully to her feet. Her husband had left in a rage. It was time. If she didn't get out soon, she knew the day would come when she could no longer rise to her feet and leave. Her endurance was gone, but her will to live was stronger than guilt and shame.

Run! Run! Run!

Stumbling to her closet, she put together a few essentials, stuffing them into a battered bag. Grabbing her purse that held less than fifty bucks, she made her way painfully back to the living room, stopping as she heard heavy steps in the hallway.

Was he back? Please let it not be him.

Holding her breath, she waited until the footfalls passed her door, her entire body trembling with relief as she released the breath in a rush, and put a shaky hand on the doorknob. She took the keys from her purse and dropped them on the table beside the door, a symbol to herself that she was never coming back. Whatever happened to her in the future had to be better than her past.

She was alone.

She was damaged.

She was broke, with less than fifty dollars to her name.

And she was afraid.

But none of those things was going to deter her now. Taking one last, quick glance around the apartment, she acknowledged that nothing here belonged to her anyway, and it had never been home. It had been her hell, her prison. She had nothing to lose. She'd find a way to make a new life for herself.

Survive! Survive! Survive!

The woman fled and never looked back, hoping to leave her painful history behind her.

Chapter 1

Kade Harrison had always liked games. He might even have to say that he lived and breathed just to engage in almost any type of sporting event. It was the one thing he was good at—the only thing at which he'd ever excelled—and he didn't like to lose. Unfortunately, he'd been losing for the last two months, and it was really beginning to piss him off.

Where the hell is she?

Tracking down Asha Paritala had almost become a competitive sport. Kade had been working on cornering Asha for two months, traveling from one side of the country to the other, only to come up empty-handed every single time. He was losing this particular contest, and he didn't like it. The woman was smart, ditching him before he could quite catch up with her. Kade had no doubt he and Asha were playing a game of cat and mouse, and she was avoiding him. God knew he'd left enough messages in various places that she must have gotten at least one of them. She was evading him for some unknown reason, but the cat was going to pounce. Just as soon as he could corner the cagey little mouse.

Letting himself into his Nashville hotel room, Kade pulled off his baseball cap and collapsed on the king-sized bed with a sigh. He'd have to call his brother-in-law, Max, and let him know that he'd failed...again. Asha had just left the homeless shelter a few minutes before he had arrived, and no one there had any idea where she was headed. She'd left her few meager belongings behind, so Kade had some hope she'd return, but nobody at the shelter really knew her, and nobody seemed quite certain where she was or if she would be coming back.

All's fair in pursuit and winning this game. Newsflash, little mouse: I can fight dirty. You know where your stuff is...come and get it.

Grinning, Kade rolled over on the bed and grabbed up the bag with Asha's belongings, only wrestling with his conscience for a moment about taking her things and leaving her a message where they could be picked up. He'd give them back if and when she showed up. In the meantime, he'd use any clue he could find to figure out exactly who she was and if there was any chance she was a lost sibling to Max. He'd wasted two months getting this favor done—tracking down a woman he didn't know, a woman who could possibly be related to Max—and he was going to bring it to an end. Although his twin, Travis, did most of the work in Tampa for the Harrison Corporation, Kade did have *some* responsibilities that he'd insisted on taking over once his football career had ended, and he eventually needed to get back to Tampa.

He grimaced as he stretched his body out on the bed. His lame right leg was aching from two months of nonstop searching for a woman who he was beginning to think was nothing more than a phantom, an illusion. But he knew Asha Paritala existed, that she was real, and he was determined to find her. Maddie and Max deserved to know if this woman was their sister. Never mind that he hadn't even gotten one tiny glimpse of Asha. He would. Soon. In some ways, he almost didn't want the search to end. He'd felt more alive in the last two months than he had since his accident. Matching wits with the unknown female was a challenge, and there was nothing Kade loved more than winning a difficult game. Gut instinct told him that she knew he was looking for her. The question was...why was she running away? It wasn't like he wanted anything except information from her, and it could gain her two siblings who she'd never known existed. There weren't many people who *wouldn't* want to be related to Max and Maddie, seeing as they were two of the richest people in the world— in addition to being two of the kindest individuals Kade knew.

"I'm not sure why I'm so damn impatient. It isn't like I have anything else to do until Travis needs me," he said to himself grimly, admitting that his twin rarely called on him for anything, and Travis never *needed* anyone. And it had left Kade feeling useless, restless. His days as a pro football player were over. His stint as a star quarterback for the Florida Cougars was nothing more than a memory, the one thing he loved having been torn away from him almost two years ago when a drunk driver had failed to see him on his motorcycle. His leg had been mangled all to hell when the inebriated idiot had moved into his lane and caught Kade's leg between his truck and Kade's bike. He didn't remember much of the accident. But one of the first things he remembered with crystal clarity was waking up in the ICU, his longtime girlfriend, Amy, frowning at him as though he'd disappointed her. And obviously…he had. She'd dumped him right then and there, letting Kade know in no uncertain terms that she refused to be with a cripple who wouldn't be a celebrity anymore.

Trying to slam his mind shut on the unpleasant and painful memories of his accident, he focused on the belongings he'd dumped on the bed: a few articles of worn clothing, a hairbrush, a toothbrush that had definitely seen better days, a large pad of paper and some well-used charcoal blocks and pencils. Pushing the other articles aside, he opened the pad of paper, mesmerized as he slowly flipped the pages, studying each drawing before going to the next.

Each image nearly leaped from the page, so real that it almost seemed as if they could jump from the paper and come to life in front of him. The drawings were fanciful—many of them looking like mythological creatures or animals—in the first part of the collection.

She's an artist. A fucking amazing artist.

"Damn," he whispered in an awed voice as he skipped some blank pages and came to another section, revealing her portraits. He didn't recognize any of the individuals she had drawn. Obviously, they were ordinary people going about their daily activities, but he could feel every emotion on a drawing of an elderly woman's face, a woman who looked like she was sitting on a bench at a bus stop, and he could almost share the joy of a group of children playing on a playground. Flipping through the rest of the pictures of people, he was dumb-struck by Asha's talent. He was no artist, but the drawings could touch even *his* emotions, and he wasn't a particularly emotional type of guy.

Kade felt his mouth go dry, and his gut lurched as he revealed the last picture, a man and a woman poised to engage in a passionate embrace. The male's face was shaded, his head turned to the side, but the woman's desire was so potently drawn that he could feel her naked longing, her desperation as she waited for the man she was embracing to kiss her. Long, silky hair cascaded down her back, her head tilted for his kiss, her face revealing unguarded need.

The words scrolled beneath the drawing hit Kade with a visceral reaction:

Someone! Someday! Somewhere!

Damned if Kade didn't want to be the mystery man in shadow, the guy to kiss the woman breathless, provide the passion he could sense she desperately wanted. He knew exactly how she felt; he'd felt the same way. In fact, he *still* felt like that every time he saw his little sister Mia and her husband Max together, or his friends, Sam and Maddie, and Simon and Kara. All of them had found their mates, the person who made them feel whole, and the happiness that surrounded those couples was almost ball-bustingly painful for a man like him who felt so alone, so solitary. He was damned happy for all of them—every one of them deserved to be happy—but it wasn't easy not to feel lost, not to mention a little odd, when he was around them. He just didn't roll that way, and he kept his emotions in check. He'd been conditioned to keep a grip on himself since he was a child, and he'd learned to keep a handle on himself throughout his football career. It was too vital for him to stay cool and detached. Letting his emotions rule him would have meant mistakes, and he'd rarely made errors when he was on a football field. Besides, a guy coming from a father as crazy as his had to have control. He and his siblings had all tried to never do anything that could be misconstrued as the least bit emotional or out of the ordinary. It was their way of trying to separate themselves from their sire.

Kade sighed heavily and continued to stare at the picture, wondering what it was like to feel that type of passion. Yeah. Sure. He liked sex. What guy didn't? But the desire was short-lived and easily resolved. Granted, he hadn't had to resolve *that* problem for two years. There was something about nearly losing a leg and two years of grueling rehabilitation that pushed that particular desire onto the back burner.

The woman's not real. It's just a picture.

Kade closed the drawing pad with more force than necessary, disgusted with himself. He'd never been a romantic sort of guy. He was a jock. He'd been with Amy since college, and she'd hated open displays of affection. The only things she'd ever really liked were the expensive gifts he'd lavished on her and the extravagant parties he was forced to attend because of his celebrity status and endorsements. And now that he was lame, he wasn't the type of guy to ever have a woman look at him like he was the only man in the world for her, wealthy or not. Not that any woman ever *had* looked at him that way, even before he'd fucked up his leg. He was, after all, one of those crazy Harrisons with the old man who had offed his own wife. Although a woman might appreciate his monetary assets, he was fairly certain no woman would covet *him*. He was damaged goods, unable to ever play football again—the one thing that had made him feel valuable. He might have money, but that was about *all* he had to give anymore. Honestly, maybe it had always been that way for him; maybe he just wasn't capable of having a woman who felt that way about him. He wasn't exactly *any* woman's ideal of a knight in shining armor and he was pretty doubtful that he was entitled to own that kind of love. He'd had a batshit crazy old man who beat up his kids and his wife often, and his father had eventually killed Kade's mother, and then himself. Was there ever a happily ever after for a fucked-up and dysfunctional family like his? Mostly, all he, Travis, and Mia had concentrated on was survival.

Mia found her happily ever after with Max. She's happy now.

Kade released a heavy breath and stuffed Asha's meager belongings back into her bag. His younger sister, Mia, *was* happy. But her road to bliss had been pretty damn rocky. His sibling deserved every bit of happiness she now had with her husband, Max. God knew she'd suffered dearly for it.

Kade wished his older twin, Travis, could find some peace, but Kade knew that he and Travis shared the same darkness, a dimness of their souls that would probably always keep them isolated and alone. Travis wore his blackness like a mantle; Kade tried to hide his own. But it was still there, the yawning, dark emptiness that never went away; his accident had only made it worse, blacker and emptier than it had ever been before. His football career had kept him busy, given him a purpose. Without that, there was nothing that stood between him and the shadowy memories of his past.

I'm different. I'm just not cut out for a relationship any deeper than what I had with Amy.

He'd always known his relationship with Amy had been superficial, but it had always suited both of them. What the hell did he know about love? He was fairly certain he wasn't even capable of really loving a woman. Since his break-up with Amy, he'd been alone. Strangely, he didn't feel much different than when he was in the relationship. Her cruel words had hurt, but had he really expected anything different? He'd broken all the unspoken rules of their relationship when he'd had his accident, and his recovery had taken close to two years. Had he really expected her to stick it out with him, to stay by his side when everything had changed? Amy was a beautiful supermodel, and she hadn't signed on to take care of a critically ill man and then two years of rehabilitation. She'd wanted the parties, the expensive presents, the recognition of being the girlfriend of a famous quarterback, a man who didn't walk with a limp and count his blessings every damn day that he actually still *had* his right leg. Not surprisingly, she'd taken up with another rising star quarterback soon after his accident—ironically, one he'd introduced her to at a party—and never looked back.

Kade rolled off the bed and stood up, telling himself that it didn't really matter. He'd always had Travis and his friends while he was recovering. The rehab was over and his life was moving on. He had Mia back in the family fold again after having gone missing for two years, and he had a favor to do for Max—a favor that he was determined to see through to the very end. Kade knew that Max would be haunted by not knowing if Asha was his lost sibling or not, so he'd agreed to go find Asha Paritala and discover the truth. It wasn't like he had much else to do since his days as a quarterback were over, and the distraction had been a good one, something he'd desperately needed.

I needed something to take my mind off the fact that I'll never play football again. Kade was dealing with that reality, rationalizing every single day to accept it. So what if he missed his football career as much as he would miss the air that he breathed if it were suddenly taken away? It wasn't as if he could have played football forever. He just wished he hadn't had to end a career he'd loved so abruptly and so damn soon. He'd only been thirty years old, and still would have had a lot of good years ahead of him. And he'd been a good quarterback. Damn good. Football had been a very big part of his life for so long that he felt like he was just drifting now, as though he wasn't quite sure what he *should* be doing. He owned Harrison Corporation along with Travis, but his twin had run Harrison so smoothly when Kade was playing football, that he now felt unneeded in his own company. Travis liked control, and Kade really had no reason not to give it to him. His brother spent most of his time in the Harrison offices, but it was by choice, a diversion for Travis. They had competent upper management, and Travis didn't need to spend every waking moment in the office, but it was his brother's way of controlling his life, burying the pain of his past in work.

Kade knew he was really no different than Travis, football always being his escape, even when he was a kid. Winning a college football scholarship to play in Michigan had been one of the best things that had ever happened to him at the age of eighteen, taking him far away from the craziness of his life in Tampa. He'd come back to Florida to play as a pro because they'd made the best offer, but he'd spent half of his time on the road and the other half practicing. He'd purchased a beautiful home in Tampa years ago, but he'd rarely spent any time there until he'd had his accident. Amy had lived her own life in a luxury condo that Kade had paid for, refusing to take up residence with him unless he married her. Now, he was pretty sure that she was thanking her lucky stars that he hadn't been ready for marriage.

Walking to the mini-bar, Kade reached into the small fridge and pulled out a beer. Screwing off the top, he took a large swig and thumbed through the room service menu. He was starving, and he managed to order up about half the menu items before he finished placing his order.

Restless, he took a quick shower and changed into a worn pair of jeans and an orange buttoned-down shirt with dancing rabbits of various colors decorating the material. Kade smiled, knowing Travis would hate his new shirt and Mia would tease him to death about it, but he didn't care. He'd started out wearing gaudy shirts when he was an adolescent to amuse Mia. Living in their family madness, Kade would have done just about anything to make his little sister smile, since there had been very little to smile about when they were kids. Now, he wore the shirts because he actually liked them. They had become a part of him over the years, a small thing that seemed to lighten some of the shadows inside him. The guys on the team had ribbed him endlessly, but if there was one thing that Kade *wasn't* insecure about, it was his manhood. He basically told them all to kiss his ass and wore whatever he wanted to make himself happy. After a while, his teammates had seen his attire as a source of entertainment, every one of them waiting to see what he'd wear next so they could give him hell about it. Really, Amy had been the only one who truly hated them, and she'd refused to be seen with him unless he was dressed in what she considered "normal clothes."

Kade was just reaching for another beer when there was a knock on his door. Chucking the beer top in the trash, he took a long slug of his drink, fumbled with the bolt on the door and swung it open.

He froze, every muscle in his body seizing up all at once. He wasn't sure how long he stood there, drowning in the chocolate-dark, wide eyes staring back at him from the doorway. Kade was stunned, his heart rate accelerating until it was pounding in his ears, the air leaving his lungs in a heavy *whoosh*, feeling like he'd taken a hard kick to the gut after a particularly rough quarterback sack.

Definitely *not* his food arriving from room service!

Kade had no doubt that the woman in front of him was Asha Paritala, but she wasn't at all what he'd expected. She was dressed in a tie-dye shirt, the orange almost matching the shade he was wearing. Teal and green intermingled with the tangerine color of her top, making her look like an exotic flower. Long, flowing blue-black hair fell below her shoulders and down her back—straight, beautiful, and making him itch to reach out and touch it to see if it was as silky as it appeared. Her creamy skin was such a contrast to her dark hair and eyes that she looked like an exotic wet dream.

He had an instant hard-on as the scent of jasmine surrounded him, making him hard enough to cut through steel. She moved cautiously into the room when he held the door wider.

"Asha?" he croaked, his mouth still dry, his adrenaline beginning to course through his body. She was average height for a woman, but he dwarfed her. Still, she looked fragile, like the slightest breeze would blow her away. Obviously, her looks were deceptive. After all, she'd led him on a merry chase for the last two months.

"What do you want?" she asked impatiently, her eyes flashing dark fire.

Kade closed the door. *You! I want you underneath me, on top of me, or any other way you want it.* Aloud, he answered, "My name is Kade Harrison. I've been looking for you. Didn't you get my messages?"

Ignoring his question, she answered, "You stole my things. You're a thief." Her tone was hostile, but her expression still showed her apprehension.

"I'm not a thief. I was desperate and trying to get you to talk to me. And I wouldn't have left my contact information if I was trying to rip you off," Kade answered defensively. Honestly, he was *still* desperate, only now it was a whole different kind of desperation. His libido, which had been running low while he was recovering from his accident, had finally awakened with a vengeance and taken complete control of his body.

She went and picked up her tattered cloth bag, hefting it over her shoulder after checking the contents. She stopped right in front of him, her deep brown eyes angry, but also showing a hint of vulnerability and fear. "Just tell me why you've been following me. Are you some kind of crazy stalker?"

Kade felt his anger rise up at the thought of anyone causing this woman distress, and some personal annoyance that Asha obviously thought he was some kind of psycho. "No. Is someone stalking you?"

Their eyes locked, and she searched his face, as though she were looking for the truth. "I don't know," she answered honestly. "But I know someone has been following me. I'm assuming it's been you. And yeah, I got some messages that didn't make any sense to me. Did you really expect me to answer you? I don't even know you. What do you want from me?"

It was a loaded question that he could have answered in many different ways because of the unusual response his body was having to her presence, but none of them were quite appropriate at the moment. More than likely, any one of the answers that came immediately to mind would have her running away screaming. Kade dug into his pocket and pulled out his wallet, chagrined that he'd frightened her by following her. She'd been running away from fear, a woman alone who didn't like an unknown guy following her. It had never occurred to him that she might be scared of him, and for some reason, he didn't like that thought. Holding up a picture of Maddie and Max, he said, "It was me. I'm doing a favor for friends. We think there's a possibility that you could be related to my brother-in-law and his sister. I've been trying to track you down for almost two months. I'm not trying to hurt you. I just wanted to talk to you."

Asha put her fingertip on the picture and traced it slowly. "These two people?" She sighed. "Do I look like I'm related to these two? My mother was a Caucasian American, but my father was an Indian immigrant. I don't look anything like these two people. I can tell they're related. They look a lot alike." A brief look of regret and sadness flickered in the depths of her dark eyes.

"They have the same mother and father. There's a chance that they could be your half-siblings, related on your mother's side," Kade answered, his heart clenching as he saw the wistful expression on her face. She was trying to put on a brave front, but she looked so weary, so alone, and it made him want to shelter her from anything and everything that made her feel that way. He wondered when she'd last eaten a good meal or slept for a decent length of time.

Looking away from the picture and dropping her hand, she pierced him with a doubtful look. "That's not possible. There's no way I'm related to them. Please leave me alone," she answered sadly and dejectedly as she headed for the door.

Kade grasped her upper arm before she could make any forward progress. "Don't you want to know for sure? What if you *are* related?"

Shrugging her arm away from him, she answered, "I'm Indian."

"But you were born here? To an American mother?"

"An American mother and an Indian father who I can't even remember," she agreed, her body starting to tremble. "I was born here, but my foster parents were from India. I was raised as an Indian."

Kade had felt the heat of her body through the thin material of her shirt. "Are you okay?" He lifted a hand to her face, only to find it burning hot. "You have a fever."

She's undernourished, exhausted...and ill. Fuck! Doesn't she have anyone out there who gives a shit about her?

"I'm fine," she replied weakly. "I'm just a little under the weather. And it's been a long day."

Bullshit. She's sick. I can see her starting to sweat, and she looks like she's about ready to keel over.

"You're sick." Kade put an arm around her waist to steady her.

She moaned softly, leaning her weight against his body as though she wasn't able to stand without help. "I need to go. I can't be sick."

"You're staying," Kade answered hotly. There was no way he was letting her walk out the door in her condition. She'd be on the floor before she ever left the hotel.

She wiggled out of his grip and headed unsteadily for the door, Kade hot on her heels.

She opened the door and turned to look at him, her eyes bright with tears and probably fever. "Please. Just leave me alone. My life is difficult enough right now. I can't deal with anything else. I'm not related to those people in the picture, and I wish you'd stop following me."

Kade opened his mouth to reply, but he stopped short as her body began crumpling to the ground. He caught her just in time, scooping her into his arms and slamming the door closed. Taking her to the big bed, he laid her on the comforter. Staring down at her, he realized two things immediately: she was very sick, and *this* was the woman in that unsettling drawing he had seen in her collection. It had been a self-portrait, a woman pouring out her own emotions on a drawing pad.

"Fuck," Kade uttered irritably, realizing that Asha wasn't really very coherent. Her eyes were closed and her body was as limp as a wet noodle. Her thin shirt was drenched with perspiration, and her skin was fiery hot.

Her eyes flickered open momentarily, and she squinted at him, as though she were slightly confused. "I love your shirt. It's so… happy and colorful," she murmured softly, attempting a weak smile. "I really need to go now. I have things to do," she said groggily, her voice lacking conviction.

Kade would have smiled if he wasn't so panicked about having a woman this sick on his bed. She was as weak as a kitten and he doubted she could even get to the edge of the bed without help. He admired her tenacity, but she wasn't going anywhere on her own steam.

"Yeah, we *are* going," Kade answered, wrapping her now trembling body in a blanket from the bed. "To the hospital." He might be able to do minor first aid on sports injuries, but he had no idea what to do with a woman as sick as Asha was at the moment.

Her eyes flew open wide, her expression now panicked and her teeth chattering. "I c-can't g-go there—it's expensive..." Her voice trailed off as she started coughing so hard that it rocked her fragile body.

Fuck! She's sick as hell, and all she's worried about is the expense?

Her illness scared the shit out of him. In fact, it terrified him almost as much as the possessive, protective instincts he was experiencing as he realized how vulnerable she was at the moment. But mostly, it bugged the hell out of him that she was actually frightened. He didn't ever want this woman to be scared of him or anything else on the planet. Why...he wasn't quite certain, but he'd leave that mystery for another time. All he wanted at that very moment was to see her well and healthy. In fact, the need to get her that way was about to become an obsession.

He lifted her, blanket and all, and hauled her off to the hospital.

Chapter 2

Asha came awake slowly, her head foggy and her entire body aching. Blinking several times to clear her vision, she tried to remember where she was and what had happened to her. Strangely, all she could remember was Kade.

Kade…forcing her to wake up to give her medication.

Kade…plying her with fluids.

Kade's reassuring voice as she fell asleep, so exhausted she couldn't keep her eyes open.

Asha tried to scramble into a sitting position, looking frantically around the room, her heart thundering as she realized she was still in Kade's very nice hotel room.

What the hell am I doing here?

Crawling to the edge of the massive bed, she started to cough as she swung her feet over the edge, making her grasp her sore ribs as she continued hacking and barking. "Damn it!" she choked between coughs. Bending at the waist, she held her side, wincing from the soreness of her ribs and abdomen, the muscles strained from coughing.

I can't afford to be sick right now. Survive! Survive! Survive!

"What the hell are you doing?" Kade's angry voice sounded from across the room.

He brought her a glass of water and some pills. She swallowed them compliantly, not even asking what they were. She felt too horrible to care, and he'd already had the chance to kill her if he was some sort of crazed lunatic. If the pills would make her feel better, she'd swallow anything he gave her.

"You can't get up yet," Kade told her in the voice of a dictator, taking the empty glass from her hand. "You have pneumonia."

"I need to use the bathroom," she told him, embarrassed, but the need to pee was so urgent that she couldn't wait.

Kade didn't say a word. He scooped up her body remarkably gently for a guy who had a body built like a Mack truck, and took her to the bathroom, plopped her on the toilet seat, folded his arms and lifted a brow. "Go."

Asha looked up at him. "Seriously? You expect me to go with you standing right here?" No way was *that* happening. She was dressed in her threadbare nightgown with no panties, clothing she must have donned after their visit to the hospital, but she didn't remember doing it. The memories of the emergency room were slowly coming back to her, but everything was pretty hazy. "I can't pee with you watching me." Having this conversation, this experience with a man she barely knew was mortifying, but she was in a desperate situation where she had little choice but to be blunt. Her bladder was ready to explode, and she was trying desperately not to cough.

Kade grinned and turned his back. "Okay. Now go. I shared a locker room with plenty of guys. It was close quarters and I've heard plenty of men take a piss. I'm sure it sounds pretty much the same with a female."

"I'm not one of the guys. Leave," she insisted, grinding her teeth with the need to relieve her herself.

"Not happening. You're too weak and you're likely to fall. You're sick, Asha. And I just gave you something for your cough and the pain that will probably just make you loopier. I'm not leaving."

To tell the truth, she was weak, dizzy, and miserable. Still, how could a woman use the bathroom with a man she didn't know standing right in front of her? Finally, the needs of her body won out and she quickly did her business, and rose, needing to grab onto the waistband of Kade's jeans to keep herself upright.

He had her in his arms quicker than she could blink, cradling her against his muscular chest, strong arms enveloping her, making her feel safer than she'd felt...well...ever. How could she feel so vulnerable and yet so safe at the same time?

"Wait. I need to wash my hands," she told him weakly.

"You have to worry about good hygiene now?" Kade rolled his eyes, but he stopped patiently at the sink, testing the water temperature before he let her put her hands under the faucet. He dried her hands like she was a child and proceeded back to the bedroom at a fast stride for a man who limped.

After he'd tucked her back into bed, she asked softly, "What time is it?"

Kade sat on the edge of the bed, answering, "You came here yesterday afternoon. It's now..." He glanced at his watch. "Eight o'clock in the evening. You slept all last night and all day."

"Oh, no! I had a job today. I have to make a call." She really needed the money from the job, and she had to call and reschedule. Losing the income was not an option, and her fear and survival instincts were beating at her. For so many years, one word had pounded through her brain unceasingly: *Survive. Survive. Survive.* "I needed that job, and now I have to pay for the hospital visit and the medicine."

"What kind of job?" Kade asked curiously. "The hospital has already been paid and I have all the medication you need. You don't owe anything."

"Then I need to pay you," she told him adamantly. Her purse was at the bedside, and she stretched for it, grabbing it up and rifling through the contents. "I paint walls," she answered distractedly, still looking for the piece of paper with the client's number.

"What kind of walls?"

Triumphant, she pulled out the paper with the number, snatching some photos from the side pocket of her bag with her other hand. "Any wall that a person wants painted." She handed him the photos. "I'll pay you as much as I can before I go and I'll have to send you the rest. I'm sorry. That's my only option." There was nothing else she could do since she didn't have the money to pay him back completely. "Can I use your phone?" Her cell had quit working a few weeks ago, and finding a pay phone in a world where everyone had a cell phone was nearly impossible. She'd had to scramble to find a way to connect with jobs. She used the Internet in the public libraries to check her website and corresponded by email. But calling clients was rarely possible since she'd lost her phone. It might have been a cheap prepaid, but it was her connection to jobs, and the loss was making her scramble even harder to communicate with people who wanted her services.

"Incredible," Kade said as he flipped through the photos. "You do art on walls?"

Asha shrugged. "I can do designs on anything, but I mostly do walls."

"So you travel around the country, painting walls? How do people find you?"

"I have a website. Designs by Asha. They usually contact me from there. I get a lot of repeat clients and referrals."

Kade finished looking at the pictures and handed them back to her. "I'm not surprised. You do incredible work." He plucked the number from her fingers and pulled out his cell phone.

Asha watched in horror as he called her client and promptly canceled, telling the expectant mother on the other end of the line that Asha was sick and wouldn't be able to paint her nursery wall anytime soon. He hung up without getting another date or appointment.

"I can't believe you just did that," she told him with as much anger as she could muster, which wasn't much. She was too damn weak, and anger took more energy than she had at the moment. She settled for glaring at him, giving him what she hoped was an angry stare. Drowsy, she lay back on the pillow and crossed her arms in front of her.

"You're sick. You aren't doing anything except resting your gorgeous ass in my bed for a while," he informed her gruffly. "And you aren't paying me back, so quit stressing about money."

Asha opened her mouth to reply, but promptly closed it again, his personal comment about her butt rendering her speechless. No one had ever told her she had a gorgeous *anything*, and it flummoxed her into silence.

Looking up at Kade, her heart skipped a beat as she looked at his stubborn expression. His beautiful blue eyes were kind, but his look told her that he wasn't budging, and Asha had a feeling he had a stubborn streak a mile wide. She'd already discovered that he was bossy. Her eyes roamed his incredibly toned, buff body, his biceps bulging from beneath another colorful short-sleeved shirt as he crossed his arms and stared back at her, making her totally incapable of looking away. He was so handsome that it was almost painful to look at him. His eyes were as turbulent as the ocean during a storm; his hair was several different shades of blond, making him appear just a little bit wild and dangerous. He might be wearing a shirt that should have made him seem harmless, but it didn't diminish his masculinity even a tiny little bit. Well over six feet tall, Kade Harrison was solid muscle, and all male, testosterone emanating from him in gigantic waves. Asha knew his size and bulk should probably scare her. After all, she didn't even know him. Strangely, she wasn't afraid of him at all. He fascinated her. His only flaw seemed to be his limp, but having that tiny imperfection made him even more captivating, making her wonder what had happened to him. Somehow, it made him seem more human.

"I can't afford to be out of the job," Asha admitted reluctantly, feeling like a complete loser next to this man who obviously had his shit together financially. He'd paid what was probably a hefty hospital bill without thought, and the hotel he was staying in was one that didn't have average, middle-class clientele. It catered to people with money.

Kade didn't answer immediately. He held her gaze as he stretched out on the bed next to her before finally saying, "I have a proposition for you. But I don't want to talk about it right now. I just want you to work on getting well again. I won't let anything happen to you, Asha. I promise."

His low, reassuring baritone flowed over her like silk, making her want to sink into him and happily drown. No one had ever offered to protect her before. How strange and wonderful it seemed to have a complete stranger taking care of her like she was someone of value. "You must know that I'm not related to those two people in the picture. It's a lovely thought, but it's not possible. And even if it was, it isn't a priority for me. I need to survive right now."

Survive. Survive. Survive.

Kade put a finger to her lips and shook his head. "Not now. You'll survive just fine. You're safe and I'll keep you safe. Trust me."

Trust me.

Kade didn't understand her background, or how difficult it was to put her future into *anyone's* hands, no matter how tempting the idea was to her right now because she was sick and her defenses were down. She was fighting to survive, to be independent. But whether she liked it or not, she *was* completely at his mercy for the moment. She shook her head and closed her eyes. "I can't. I need to take care of things myself."

"You can trust me. I'm a trustworthy kind of guy," Kade countered stubbornly, stroking the hair away from her face. "Sleep now. The doctor said that rest was the fastest way to shake off the pneumonia."

Asha couldn't argue. She opened her eyes for a moment, but her lids were heavy and her body felt like lead. Reaching out her hand, she fingered the collar of Kade's festive shirt, red with green designs. It felt like silk. "This is beautiful. It looks good on you." The red only intensified the lightness of Kade's hair and the depth of his blue eyes. Bold, powerful colors and ornate designs suited him. Being partial to light and color herself, Kade delighted her senses.

She heard Kade laugh before answering, "I always said if I ever found a woman who actually likes my shirts, I'd marry her."

Asha wanted to answer, wanted to tell Kade never to marry unless his whole heart was engaged. She'd been in a loveless marriage, and she'd never felt more alone. Her eyes fluttered closed again before she could answer, the drugs and pure exhaustion finally dragging her into a dreamless sleep.

"Do you need us to come and talk to her?" Max Hamilton asked, his voice coming from Kade's phone, which was on speaker as Kade shaved with the bathroom door closed. He didn't think Asha would wake up anytime soon.

"No. She's sick. I'll talk to her as soon as she's well enough to travel," Kade answered protectively. The last thing Asha needed was a three-ring circus with all her possible relatives coming to Nashville to talk to her.

"Is she okay?" Max asked, concerned.

"Yeah. I think so. She'll recover. I don't know her whole story, but her life hasn't been easy, Max." Asha obviously traveled from place to place, making just enough money to get her to her next job. She had nothing, yet there was a sweetness about her that had Kade on edge every moment he was near her...and every moment when he wasn't. What kind of life had she known? Everything she owned fit in one small bag and her purse. "I'll get more information in a few days. She needs to rest and recover right now."

Max's deep sigh came through the phone line. "Get her well, Kade. Take care of her."

Kade intended to do just that, and not because she might be Max's half-sister. His possessive instincts were all his own. "She likes my shirts," he told Max jokingly, wiping his shaven face with a towel.

"She needs her vision checked," Max answered drily. "What's she like? Does she look like Maddie?"

Kade paused for a moment, tossing the towel into the laundry pile. "No. She doesn't look like either one of you, but she's beautiful. Her father was an Indian immigrant, but that doesn't mean you can't still be related. Her mother was American."

"Does she have a birth certificate?" Max asked, obviously anxious to find out more about Asha.

"I don't know. We didn't have a chance to talk much about her past before she almost did a nosedive to the carpet. She collapsed almost from the moment I met her. Let me get her well, Max," Kade answered irritably, not happy that Max didn't seem to understand his main priority was to get Asha healthy. "I'll get her to come to Tampa."

"Thanks," Max answered gratefully. "I don't mean to push. I guess I'm just anxious to know. I'm glad you finally found her. I owe you."

Kade was glad too, but for totally different reasons than seeing if Asha was related to Max. "I'll remember you said that. I'll keep in touch. I'll get her to Florida as soon as I can."

"How's your leg holding up?" Max asked, the concern in his voice evident.

"It's fine." Actually, it ached like hell, but Kade wasn't about to admit it.

He hastily ended his conversation with Max before his brother-in-law could pry any further. Or worse yet, put Mia on the phone to try to wangle more information out of him.

Stepping out of the bathroom, Kade's eyes went instantly to the bed. Asha was still sleeping, but she was tossing restlessly. The sheets were tangled, thrown from her body, probably during a period when her fever had made her overly warm. He climbed onto the bed, touching the back of his hand to her cheek. Her face was slightly damp, but cool, her fever probably under control from the drugs he had given her before she'd fallen asleep.

Her body started to shiver, and Kade grabbed the sheets and blankets that had been kicked to the bottom of the bed. As he went to draw them back up, his eyes caught a small patch of red on the top of her right foot. Looking closer, he could see that it was actually an intricate pattern, a stylized butterfly trying to emerge from the confines of its cocoon. Kade knew tattoos, and as he traced the pattern lightly with his fingers, he wondered exactly what it meant. It was henna, the rendering already lightened with age, but he could still make out every detail.

"Ow! Shit!" Kade quickly jerked his fingers away and moved back as Asha drew back her foot and kicked him in his bum leg. Her eyes were still closed, and she was still asleep. The action had been reflexive, a subconscious reaction to his touch, but it still hurt like hell. Rubbing his leg, he moved back to the head of the bed.

Asha tossed her head, her hair sliding along the fine cotton of the pillow. "I need to get out! I need to get out! I can't do this anymore." Her voice was raw and frightened.

Kade quickly shucked his clothes, leaving on his silk boxers, and slid into the bed beside Asha. Her panicked, scared ramblings tugged at him, lured him closer. She could go ahead and kick him again. He didn't give a shit. All he wanted to do was comfort her, make her feel safe. The need to shelter her from anything unpleasant was stronger than his physical pain, and Asha tapped into emotions that Kade hadn't even known he possessed.

"Kade?" Asha murmured softly as he gathered her close to him and covered them both with the blankets, his arm wrapping around her waist. She squirmed until her head was resting comfortably against his shoulder. "I need you," she murmured softly.

Kade's heart squeezed and he gulped. Hard. Those three little words undid him, as did the soft sigh that came from her lips as she melted into his body. Her breathing evened out, and her body relaxed, trusting him to keep her safe as she slept.

I need you.

When was the last time anyone had ever needed *him*? His grip on her tightened reflexively, his need to protect her so strong that he had to force himself not to clutch her too hard.

Asha Paritala was still a mystery to him, yet he was drawn to her as he'd never been drawn to a woman before in his entire life. She burrowed into his side, seeking his body heat, nearly making him groan with frustration. He wanted her closer, yet he needed to move away to keep his sanity. She tested his control in ways that scared the shit out of him. When she sprawled on top of him, he gritted his teeth, but his arms wrapped around her and cradled her body over his, knowing he'd warm her. His body was on fire, and probably throwing off heat like a furnace. The thin nightgown she was wearing was an ineffective barrier between them, but Kade still wanted it gone. He wanted to be skin-to-skin with this woman in the worst way.

She's sick. She's vulnerable.

Those thoughts made him grip her just a little bit tighter.

I need you.

He could still hear her words echoing through his head in her husky, plaintive voice. Inhaling deeply, he let her jasmine scent fill every one of his senses.

She's mine!

Kade shook his head at his wayward thoughts, but the gnawing in his gut just kept getting stronger. Every primitive instinct inside his body was screaming that this woman belonged with him. It was like everything had clicked into place—*she* had clicked into place— joining them together in an irrevocable way.

I don't even fucking know her.

Problem was, something inside of him *did* recognize her, a part of himself that had been aching to find something or someone to relieve his emptiness. For the first time in forever, he wanted to stop running and enjoy the sensation of the woman in his arms, be intoxicated by her scent. Even though his body was clamoring to have her carnally, he also felt…at peace.

Kade shut down his brain and simply enjoyed the feel of her body on top of his, her slim, naked legs entwining with his more muscular limbs. He couldn't shake the sense of rightness, and he wasn't sure he wanted to lose it. Needing to investigate the strange reaction he felt toward her, Kade decided a few things then and there:

One: Asha was coming back to Tampa with him, even if he had to take her kicking and screaming to do it.

Two: He didn't give a shit whether she was related to Max and Maddie or not.

Three: Once she was well, he was going to fuck her until neither one of them could move.

Four: For the first time in his life, he was going to become a hero, slaying every dragon and demon that plagued her.

Five: He was going to make her smile…a lot. Her stoic demeanor told him she hadn't had much to smile about in her life.

One arm around her waist and one hand palming her ass possessively to keep her in place, Kade fell asleep quickly, and without his usual restlessness. In fact, he was almost content.

Chapter 3

K ade didn't let her get out of bed for several days, much to Asha's dismay. After the antibiotics kicked in, she started to feel better, and being idle wasn't easy for her. The last two years had been a frantic race just to stay fed and find a bed to rest, and lying around didn't feel right to her. And she really hated being dependent on anyone. She'd been subjected to the will of others her entire life, and was just starting to get a taste of being free. Granted, she was barely staying afloat, but she was just starting to become solvent. If she could just keep getting regular jobs, put some money away, she could get a little place somewhere to call her own. *Finally!*

Survive. Survive. Survive.

"What are you doing?" The deep baritone startled Asha. She guiltily slammed her drawing book closed and shoved it into her bag beside the bed.

Not wanting to admit she was drawing a picture of him, she answered Kade vaguely. "Drawing. How was your business?"

Kade had left the hotel room several hours ago, claiming he needed to take care of some business, but not before he'd made sure she had his cell phone number to contact him if she needed him. He smiled at her as he nudged the door closed with one powerful shoulder, his arms filled with bags and packages. She smiled back at him weakly, unable to keep herself from responding to his presence. How was it possible that she'd missed him? She barely knew the guy and he'd only been gone for a few hours.

Don't do this to yourself, Asha. Don't fill your head with nonsense about Kade. He's helping you because he's kind. Just be grateful for his kindness, pay him back, and move on.

Kade's grin grew broader as he dumped the packages on the bed and asked jokingly, "Did you miss me?"

Yes!

To evade answering his question directly, she said as casually as she could manage, "It was peaceful. No one to boss me around."

No one to fuss over me. No one to talk to or argue with.

It had been too quiet. She was getting used to the sound of his voice. Even when he sang off-key in the shower with more enthusiasm than talent, he made her smile.

"I don't boss you around. I just keep you from doing anything detrimental to your health," Kade answered indignantly as he plopped on the edge of the bed.

Asha noticed him absently rubbing his right leg. "It hurts?"

Kade frowned, yanking his hand away as he answered, "It's fine. Just habit."

"It's more than that. I can tell. You're in pain. Don't you have pain medicine for when it's bad?"

"I don't use it," Kade snapped.

Asha drew back at the fierceness in his voice. "I'm sorry. It's none of my business. I was just concerned."

Kade sighed, looking instantly contrite. "I used it a lot when I first got hurt. Too much. I started to like the fact that it not only took away the physical pain, but blurred me mentally, too. I could see it was becoming a crutch, an escape from the reality that I'd never play football again. I was running away from reality and I knew I had to stop before it was too late."

The naked look of regret on his face made her heart bleed for him. "Football was that important to you?" She didn't need to hear his answer. Football was obviously as important to him as her art was to her, and she didn't know what she'd do if she couldn't draw and paint.

"It was everything to me," he answered sincerely. "It was the only thing I was really good at."

Asha gaped at him. "That isn't true. I'm sure there are plenty of things you're good at doing."

Kade let out a beleaguered sigh. "Okay. It's the only thing I was good at when I was vertical." He gave her a wicked grin.

She blushed, her face heating as his eyes met and held her own. She wasn't touching that comment. Something told her that he'd be much better with sexual banter than she could manage. If there was one thing she noticed about Kade, it was that he tended to avoid talking about himself, using self-deprecating humor when he wanted to avoid a particular subject. "So you stopped running away from reality?" she asked, changing the subject as quickly as possible. She definitely didn't want to talk about sex with him.

"Pretty much," he answered honestly. "I can't say I don't miss football, but I've faced the fact that I can't play anymore, and I don't take pain meds." He paused for a moment, still staring at her intensely. "Maybe someday you'll tell me why you're running."

Unable to look at him anymore, she broke eye contact as she hedged, "Who says I'm running from anything?"

"You are," he answered sanguinely, picking up the packages on the bed and plopping them beside her. "I picked you up some stuff."

"Why?" Asha asked him, confused.

Kade shrugged. "Because it's stuff you need and don't appear to have."

When she just continued to look at him dumbfounded, Kade started digging in the bags, dragging out items one by one. "You need a phone." He handed her the latest model iPhone. "And a laptop." He removed the computer from the box and set it on her lap. "You can't run a business without the basics." Tossing another bag to her, he said mischievously, "And a few other necessities. Not exactly seductive bedroom attire, but it's an appropriate nightgown since you're sick. And the jeans and shirts look like you."

Asha looked up at Kade, so shocked that she could barely speak. "I can't pay for these right now."

"They're a gift. I don't expect you to pay for them," he growled, affronted.

Pulling the nightgown from a bag—which also included new toiletries, jeans and shirts, new drawing pens and a drawing pad—she stroked the silky material. It was pretty and feminine, a beautiful pink that would cover her entire body modestly. Everything female inside her wanted to don the nightgown, feel the silk of the material caress her body and make her feel feminine. But she finally told Kade, "I can't take these things. They must have cost a fortune."

"I said it was a damn gift," he said almost angrily. "And it didn't cost a fortune. It's just a few things you need."

"I've never really had a gift," she murmured softly, continuing to stroke over the soft material of the nightgown, unable to look at Kade because her eyes were filling with tears. "And I don't even know you. I can't accept this."

"You will accept because you need them. And how is it possible that you never received a gift? Never?" Kade asked in a confused voice.

Asha shrugged, still not meeting his eyes. "I just never have."

Kade moved closer, reaching out a large hand to gently tip her chin up. "Then let me explain the protocol. You thank me sweetly and accept what I give you so you don't hurt my tender feelings." Giving her a lopsided grin, he added, "A thank-you kiss or hug would be appropriate."

Asha impatiently brushed away a tear that escaped from her eyes, staring at him in indecision. He'd helped her so much, possibly saved her life by getting her medical treatment. How could she take anything more from him? Conversely, she didn't want to hurt his feelings. Although he'd mentioned it in a joking kind of way, rejecting gifts that he'd bought for her specifically *might* hurt him. He'd looked so excited when he'd given her these gifts. "I'll pay you back," she told him, deciding it was a good compromise. She did need the items, but he'd spent way more than she'd ever be able to afford. Obviously, he liked top-of-the-line products.

"Asha...you are not paying me back. A gift doesn't require repayment. I wanted to pick these up for you. It's no big deal to me. Understand?" he answered in a low, warning voice.

"It's a lot of money. Can you afford it?" She blurted out her anxious thoughts aloud before she could censor them.

His gaze went from intense to amused. "I think I can swing it comfortably," he answered, unable to keep the laughter out of his voice.

"Be serious," she said anxiously. "I don't want to hurt you financially. You've already done so much for me, paid my hospital bills—"

"I'm a billionaire. I'm half owner of Harrison Corporation. Plus, I was a professional football player for eight years and made millions from my contracts, which I invested well."

Asha had already assumed that Kade wasn't hurting for money... but his words shocked her. "Then why are you here? Why are you helping me?" Why would someone with that much money waste any time on her?

Kade lifted a brow, a gesture that looked both questioning and admonishing at the same time. "What? Just because I have money should mean I don't do favors for friends or family? It means I should be a prick to a woman who's sick?"

Well...she hadn't meant *that*...not exactly. She let out a soft sigh and gave him an apologetic look. She was being judgmental because he was wealthy, and there was nothing she disliked more than making untrue assumptions. "I'm sorry. This whole thing just seems so unusual. I don't know any rich people, but I'd think that they wouldn't spend their time tracking down unimportant people they didn't know."

"You aren't unimportant, and I was available since I'm not able to play football anymore. Max needed to spend time with my sister or he would have come himself. It's personal to him. He wouldn't have sent an employee to talk to you."

Asha ran a hand over the laptop, admiring the shiny, new surface. How long had it been since she'd had anything brand new? She bought everything secondhand at bargain shops or thrift stores, conserving every penny. But his gifts touched her, and meant so much more than the money he'd spent. It was almost as if he was encouraging her art career by giving her the laptop, the phone, and drawing supplies. "Thank you," she finally murmured. "This means more to me than you'll ever know. But I am paying you back for my hospital bills and the medicine. I don't care how rich you are," she finished stubbornly.

"I won't take it." Kade crossed his arms and gave her an intimidating stare, a look that she was actually getting used to seeing. "You thanked me sweetly enough. I'm waiting for my kiss." He turned his head, giving her his cheek playfully.

"I don't want to infect you," she answered hesitantly.

"You won't. You've been on antibiotics long enough, and it isn't as if we haven't breathed the same air. We've slept in the same bed for days." He leaned even closer, tapping his cheek with his finger expectantly.

Asha's memory of the first several days of her illness was spotty, but relief flooded through her that she could finally touch him, and she sprang at him, throwing her arms around his neck and landing a loud, smacking kiss to his cheek. "Thank you, Kade. I'm not sure how to repay you for helping me, but I'd like to try." Where would she have been had it not been for Kade? He'd taken care of her when she was sick, sheltered her while she was recovering, and now he'd given her things that would help her get more business.

Kade wrapped his arms around her, surrounding her with his warmth. He smelled so good that Asha lingered longer than she really thought was needed for a thank-you hug. But she couldn't help herself.

Kade drew her closer and pulled her effortlessly onto his lap, resting her head against his broad shoulder and answering huskily, "That was the best thank-you I've ever received. It's all I need."

Asha sighed happily and snuggled into his muscular body, so warm and comfortable that she never wanted to move. Eventually, she'd have to give up the sense of security she felt when she was close to him. She was alone, had always been alone. But for just a little while, she let herself relax and be comforted by a man she was slowly learning to trust.

Kade had had a reputation for being one of the calmest and most focused quarterbacks to play football. He'd rarely gotten rattled on the field. Winning had been his objective, and he'd never let his emotions get in the way of that goal.

But he wasn't on a football field, and he was far from tranquil at that particular moment.

What woman Asha's age had never received a gift?

Hell, he'd been a stupid jock, but even *he* had given his girlfriend great presents and remembered her birthday. He remembered special occasions for all of his friends and relatives.

She really has been alone. Really alone.

Kade held Asha even tighter, realizing she was falling asleep against his shoulder. She was still pretty sick, but she was improving. He hadn't had any business to do in Nashville. He'd dashed out strictly to get her a few things she needed. Now, he was glad he had. Like it or not, Asha was going to learn to accept that she wasn't alone anymore. She'd have Max and Maddie.

And she'll have me.

The proprietary beast that kept rearing its head when it came to Asha was back. Admittedly, Kade wasn't sure it ever really went away. It seemed to always be there hiding just beneath the surface, and it was clawing its way out easier and easier every day if there was any threat or slight to Asha.

Kade shifted her slender weight, tucking her sleeping form back into the bed, questions forming one right after the other in his mind.

Why had she always been alone?

What kind of a life had she lived?

Hadn't anyone ever been there to take care of her?

He knew way too little about her, and it rankled. He wanted to know everything about her. She fascinated him in a way that he was pretty sure wasn't exactly sane, and that was perhaps actually a little bit obsessive.

Asha tossed restlessly in the bed, as though haunted by dreams. Kade shucked his jeans and shirt and slipped into the bed beside her. She reached for him immediately, crawling all over him to absorb his warmth. Smiling ruefully, he had to admit that he was getting used to this specific brand of torture. He'd be disappointed now if she *didn't* seek him out in her sleep.

Stroking her hair and rubbing his hand comfortingly down her back, he whispered, "I'll find out what your troubles are and take care of them. You'll never be alone again."

Asha Paritala deserved much more than the deal that fate had obviously handed her. And Kade was determined to change that destiny for her, whether she wanted his help or not.

While Asha slept, Kade started making plans, arrangements that he was determined to put in motion the very next day.

And so...he did.

Chapter 4

Two weeks later, Asha found herself standing in the middle of Kade's enormous home, terrified to touch anything. The mansion was pristine but sterile: a house that felt nothing like a home. "You really want me to do your walls?" she asked distractedly, looking at the humungous living room and shaking her head. "What single guy has white walls and white carpet?" she added, realizing too late that maybe he *wasn't* single. She had never asked, and the only thing he'd said about marriage was his joking comment about marrying a woman who liked his shirts. Even though she had spent the last few weeks with him recovering in Nashville, she knew very little about his personal life. Wanting to pay him back for everything he'd done for her, she had hesitantly agreed to his offer to decorate his walls. She owed him a debt greater than money, but she was determined to work off some of the hospital fees he'd paid for her.

Kade shrugged as he came up beside her. "I didn't decorate it. It was done by a professional and I gave her permission to do whatever she wanted. I was on the road a lot."

Asha desperately wanted to ask him why he hadn't consulted his wife, girlfriend, or significant other, but she stayed mute. It was none of her business. She was here to work. Although, she really did hope he wasn't married or involved. She'd started to have broken memories of the first few days of her recovery. And she was pretty sure she had woken up several times in the mornings, draped over Kade like he was her personal large pillow during the first few hazy days of her illness and several mornings after that. It was like she couldn't stop herself or her subconscious mind when she was sleeping. She wanted to be near him, and she sought him out. He'd treated her kindly, but still, it was more intimacy than she would ever want to have with another woman's man. "What exactly did you have in mind?"

Kade frowned. "I don't really know. I haven't spent much time here. I just know it needs some color or something."

Asha rolled her eyes, wanting to laugh at Kade's irritated look. She didn't think he had a clue what he wanted. The house was beautiful, but it definitely didn't reflect his personality. To her, Kade was light and color, a bright star in a dark night. He just didn't realize it. He'd taken care of her for the last two weeks while she'd been recovering. He'd treated her like she was someone he cared about, which was a novelty for her, and he made her smile…a lot. After offering her—almost a complete stranger—work in his home, claiming he loved the photos of the walls she'd designed, he'd transported her in a private jet to Florida.

The trip to Florida had been her first time flying, an adventure she'd never forget. But it had also made her realize how large the gulf was between her and Kade, how different their circumstances. The house he lived in just made the distance even wider. Telling her that he was rich was one thing, but seeing it once they had left his hotel was completely overwhelming.

"Can you show me the other rooms?" she requested.

Kade dragged her from room to room, giving her a workout just from traipsing through his huge home. The rest of the house was pretty much the same, black and white, with no color and nothing that personally reflected the Kade she was beginning to like more and more. She couldn't say she really understood him. He was quirky and smart, and handsome as sin, but he rarely talked much about himself. Really, he didn't talk about much except his football career. Asha was beginning to believe Kade really *did* think that the only thing he could do was play football. And it *had* been his entire life. But he was so much stronger, so much more special than he thought. She admired the strength it had taken for him to stop escaping into pain drugs and face reality. Many men in his place wouldn't have had the strength or inclination to do it.

They stopped when they finally reached the kitchen. Kade reached into the refrigerator and handed her a bottled water and grabbed a beer for himself. He did it casually, as though it was nothing that he remembered her drink of preference when he hardly knew her. Kade did that a lot, and it always astonished her. He remembered those little things about her.

"Well, what do you think?" he asked, his voice a little uncertain.

Asha watched as he tipped his head back slightly and swallowed a swig of the beer, watching the corded muscles in his neck flex as he swallowed.

I think a man should never look as sexy and hot as you do when you're just standing there drinking a beer.

"It doesn't matter what I think. It matters what you think," she answered with a slight cough, opening her bottle of water and gulping it to try to cool herself down. Kade Harrison made her edgy in a way that was uncomfortable. And it wasn't his fault. He was just too sinfully handsome and his consideration was so unusual for her that she wasn't quite sure what to make of him. He was kind when he really didn't need to be and had nothing to gain from being nice. He asked her opinion a lot. And he talked *to* her instead of *at* her. Oh, he was bossy...but only when he was worried or concerned. Kade Harrison was so different from any man she'd ever known that she still was looking for his motivations. But it seemed as if he had none. He was just being...Kade.

"You're still sick. You're coughing again," he answered huskily, his large hand reaching out to touch her face.

"I'm fine," she argued, knowing her feverishness had nothing to do with her previous illness and everything to do with *him*.

"I'm pushing you. I'm sorry. We can talk about the house later," he said contritely.

Asha backed away, his touch disconcerting. While she was sick, she'd savored every contact. But it was different now that she was well and healthy, and when he touched her, it made her yearn for much more than a comforting contact. Now that she was well, she knew how very dangerous those longings could be. "I want to get to work. I have to find a place to stay and we should work out exactly how long this will take, how many walls you'd like done," she answered in what she hoped was a professional voice, trying to control her rioting emotions.

"All of them," Kade answered, setting his beer on the kitchen table and folding his arms in front of him. "It will be a long project, and you're staying here with me. God knows I have plenty of room."

"No one else lives here?" she asked casually, although her heart was pounding and she held her breath while she waited for his answer.

"No. Just me. It's always just been me." He pulled out a chair and motioned her to sit. "You need to take it easy. Sit and tell me what your thoughts are on what I should do with the house if you're that determined to discuss it. I want your opinion."

Asha sat, staring up at Kade as he towered over her. He wanted her opinion? Why? She'd expected him to just tell her what to do and she'd do it. "The house needs to be a reflection of you. Whatever makes you feel at home."

Heaving a masculine sigh, Kade sat in the chair across from her. "I don't really know. I've spent most of my life wrapped up in my football career. I traveled, stayed in a lot of hotel rooms. I don't know shit about what makes a home. I lived and breathed football."

She released her pent-up breath before asking, "And what do you live for now that your football career is over?" With Asha knowing next to nothing about football, Kade had needed to explain exactly how the game was played while she was recovering, and what his role had been as a quarterback for the Florida Cougars. Obviously, he was a well-known athlete, and probably most people would have recognized him. But she wasn't most people, and she'd lived in a very small world up until two years ago. She could feel his sense of loss, the longing in his voice whenever he talked about his team. It made her have the crazy compulsion to hug him close and tell him that he was so much more than just a game.

His blue eyes pierced her with a confused stare. Asha could feel Kade's despair as he answered, "My friends. My brother and sister. I've learned that there are very few things that are constant in life. I was cocky, a star quarterback who had everything, and then had it ripped away in a matter of moments. I don't count on much of anything anymore." Looking away as though he'd said too much, Kade took another slug of his beer.

Asha felt a shiver run down her spine, all too aware of just how fleeting and rare happiness could be. She'd lived most of her life doing what she thought were her duties, her obligations as an Indian woman. Conflicted, she'd spiraled downward as the burdens began to chafe, wondering who she really was and what she was meant to do with her life. "Sometimes even the things you think are constant really aren't," she murmured thoughtfully.

Kade's head jerked around to look at her again, his eyes probing. "Why? Tell me what your life was like. I can guarantee you that my sister, Mia, will be paying us a visit as soon as she knows we're back. You can't go on forever denying that you're probably related to her husband. Your mother's maiden name was the same as Max's and Maddie's, and there's a good chance you're half-siblings. They're good people, Asha. You could have a lot worse people to call family."

"I don't have family," Asha cried painfully, the words coming from her aching gut.

Kade looked at her, perplexed. "You had adoptive parents—"

"Foster parents. I was taken in by an Indian family when I was three, after my natural parents died. I was fed, clothed, and raised as an Indian woman. I went to school, but I wasn't allowed to have American friends. I was married at the age of eighteen by arrangement to an Indian man who wanted to immigrate to the United States, a cousin to my foster parents," she finished breathlessly, hardly able to believe she was spilling her guts to Kade. He did that to her, made her want to tell him exactly how she felt because she knew he wouldn't judge her. It felt strange, being able to actually talk to a man about her feelings.

"Did you love him?" Kade asked huskily.

Asha lowered her eyes, staring blankly at her bottle of water and playing with the label on it nervously. "I didn't know him, didn't even meet him until we married."

"What kind of fucked-up deal is that?" Kade asked angrily. "You were sold?"

Shame washed over her as she answered in a whisper, "Not exactly. My foster parents had financial difficulties. How could I not do what they wanted? It was expected of me. They had fed and clothed me for fifteen years. They were counting on me to help them. My ex-husband Ravi's family had some money. My foster parents had debt. Ravi's family was willing to give them the money and settle their debt in exchange for his marriage to me."

"It's no different than being sold," Kade grumbled, knocking his chair over as he rose and moved around the table, taking her hand and pulling her to her feet. "No woman should feel she has to marry. Did you fall in love with him after you were married?"

Asha looked up at Kade, unable to lie to him. "No," she whispered. "We were married for seven years and I brought him nothing but disappointment."

"What?" Kade exploded. "How could you disappoint any man?"

"I was a bad bargain for him. He wanted a child, a son. And I was never able to conceive. He got checked and he was fertile. I...wasn't," she answered, agony spilling from her words. "He was a very traditional Indian man and didn't believe in divorce. But I had to leave the marriage. It wasn't...good," she whispered huskily, shuddering as she added, "I divorced him."

"And he left you destitute?" Kade asked angrily, but his touch was gentle as he clasped her by the shoulders.

"It was my choice. I didn't think past escaping. I wanted out. I had to get out." Asha finished on a sob, her heart feeling like it had been torn from her chest. Had there ever been a time in her life where she hadn't felt unwanted, unloved? If there was, she couldn't remember it. She'd been happier since her divorce—traveling from place to place, taking jobs where she could get them—than she'd ever been in her entire life. Yes, she'd been alone, scrambling to survive, but the physical and emotional pain had subsided, and she felt like she had almost regained her sanity. "My foster parents no longer speak to me. Divorce isn't something that's accepted well in Indian culture, and I didn't fulfill the agreement my foster father made with my ex-husband."

Kade backed her up against the kitchen counter, his eyes flashing blue fire. "You're a woman. A beautiful, talented woman. You aren't a possession to be sold. Fuck! What kind of man does something like that? How can any of them sleep at night not knowing whether or not you're safe and happy?"

Asha bowed her head. "I humiliated all of them. They don't care." Tears started flowing down her cheeks unchecked, her bottled-up emotions exploding from their hiding place.

Kade grasped her chin and forced her head up. His expression was fierce as he answered tightly. "No woman should ever be sold off and they had no right to expect anything from you. Their problems weren't yours. They took on the responsibility of being foster parents willingly. And they got money to take care of you. That's probably why they never adopted you. You were barely grown when they sold you off. You should have had the opportunity to live, to get an education if you wanted it. Dammit, you should have had choices!"

Asha watched Kade's ferocious expression, but she wasn't afraid. He was actually championing her, defending her rights as a woman. Unfortunately, he didn't understand Indian culture. "I might be American, but I was raised Indian, Kade. We're motivated by duty and guilt." Was that dysfunctional? Yep. But it was hard to shake the things she'd been taught as a child and a young woman. It had taken her twenty-five years to be brave enough to break from tradition and escape a horrific marriage, and it still wasn't easy. Shame and guilt still haunted her sometimes. "Since my divorce, I've tried to break free and find the American side of my heritage. But it's still difficult sometimes. I move around a lot and it's hard to make friends. I'm still learning to be an American."

Kade moved closer, crowding her, his muscular, hot body pressed against hers. His arms enfolded her as he whispered hotly against her temple, "And was it all a duty? Was being married a duty? Or did your ex love you?"

Asha shuddered, unable to keep herself from wrapping her arms around Kade's neck as her tears continued to fall. "He didn't love me. He wanted a child," she murmured against his chest. "He couldn't divorce me, but I wasn't what he wanted. He went into rages over the situation and it made the marriage difficult. Image was everything to him, and I couldn't provide him with a family."

Kade's jaw muscles were twitching, his body tensed as he said hoarsely, "Please tell me he didn't hurt you. Tell me he never laid a finger on you or blamed you."

Asha lowered her head. "I can't. It would be a lie, and you've done too much for me to lie to you. You were right. I was running away. I've been running since I left him."

"Is he threatening you? Has he contacted you?" Kade asked anxiously, his tone furious.

"I don't think he knows where I am and I doubt he cares. He contacted a few of my former clients where we lived in California looking for me, so I hid until the divorce was final and then I ran. I've been traveling ever since then," she admitted quietly. "It got bad when I started taking on jobs. He didn't want me to work outside the home."

"What about your website?"

"He didn't know," Asha admitted. "He would have put a stop to it."

Kade pulled his head back and tilted her chin to look at her face. "Tell me where he is," he demanded, his voice low and deadly. "I'll kill the bastard."

"No!" Asha exclaimed loudly. "All I want is peace. I want to forget. Please." The fact that this man would defend her made her chest tighten in gratitude, but she didn't want Kade involved in her past. "It's over. I'm free. That's all I ever wanted."

"Did you get any help?"

"I spent the time waiting for my divorce in a woman's shelter. They helped me as much as they could. I went to their counseling, but I'm still struggling to get free of my past, I guess. I took jobs out of state to get away, start again."

"Was he fucking crazy? Didn't he realize what he had?" Kade replied fiercely. "It's goddamn lonely to be with someone who doesn't give a shit, but I can't stand the fact that he actually intentionally hurt you."

Looking into his liquid blue eyes, she said hesitantly, "You sound like you know what it feels like to be with someone who doesn't care?"

"I do. My girlfriend of ten years dumped me when I was in the ICU after my accident because I wasn't what she had bargained for, because I wasn't able to fulfill *her* ideal. I do fucking know what it feels like, and it sucks. But I wasn't powerless. I had money and I had family and friends."

Asha's heartbeat accelerated and she could sense Kade's anger and the same sense of betrayal she had felt when Ravi had basically written her off and made her his target of rage because she couldn't produce a child. "Then she wasn't worthy of you. If something so superficial turned her away, then you're better off without her," Asha answered adamantly. Kade was a man worth keeping, whatever the circumstances. Didn't his ex-girlfriend understand that he was the type of man most women longed to have, a man who was constant and would care, no matter the circumstances? "You deserved so much better than that," she said sincerely, placing her palm against his whiskered jaw.

Kade's eyes turned molten and hot, his nostrils flaring as he asked hoarsely, "How do you sleep with someone whose only objective is to get you pregnant and beats you up?"

Asha shrugged uncomfortably. "I was his wife," she said matter-of-factly. "It was my duty, and if I'd refused, it would have been worse. It was usually over with pretty quickly." She didn't want to mention that she wasn't left with much of a choice. If Ravi wanted sex, he took it. The few times she'd tried to fight it, he'd almost knocked her unconscious.

"That isn't the way it's supposed to happen, sweetheart." Kade's hand left her face, his fingers sliding sensuously through her hair. "You're a woman who's meant to be savored, a woman a man wants to pleasure. There's nothing that would give me more satisfaction than to watch you come. Hard."

His words shot straight from her fluttering belly to her core, moisture flooding between her thighs as she saw the desire in his eyes. Her cheeks were red with embarrassment, but there was raw passion raging through her body, making her unable to look away from his carnal expression. "How do you watch that when it's dark?" she asked, unable to tamp down her curiosity. "He was the only man I've ever been with and it always happened quickly, with the lights off."

"Shit! Didn't he ever make you climax?" Kade brought his hand to her ass and pulled her unresisting lower body against his hardness.

Asha's mouth dropped open with need as much as surprise. He was hard and wanting, the rest of his body as hot for her as his eyes. "No," she admitted, mesmerized and unable to stay away from the unknown force that drew her to Kade. "It was dark, and it was over in a minute or two."

"Baby, you should never be taken in the dark," Kade answered, annoyed. "Do you know you look just like the picture of yourself in your portfolio? Ripe, needy, and ready to be taken and satisfied."

Asha knew exactly what picture he was talking about. "You looked at my drawings," she accused, feeling naked and exposed. That drawing was all about her yearning, her craving for something that didn't exist.

"Someone? Sometime? Somewhere?" Kade verified gruffly. "I have the answers to those questions.

"Me," he whispered hoarsely as his lips explored the sensitive shell of her ear, his hot breath making her shiver.

"Now," he added, his fingers spearing into her hair and his hand pulling her ass up harder against his engorged cock.

"Right fucking here," he finished with a masculine groan, his lips sweeping down to capture hers.

Kade's scorching mouth sucked the breath right out of her body. Asha moaned against his lips and opened automatically, her need for this, for him, insatiable. She probably *had* looked exactly like her self-portrait, because her need was intense and unstoppable, and now Kade was delivering what she wanted with every stroke of his tongue. He kissed like a man possessed, a man determined to conquer and dominate, and she responded with equal desire. Her fingers threaded in his hair and stroked down his neck, needing to touch him as much as he seemed to need to touch her. Asha felt captured, enraptured, and dominated, his hot, muscular body pressed into hers. But she reveled in it, in him. He savored her mouth, his need urgent, but his tongue explored every recess of her mouth like he needed to be acquainted with every inch of it. He vibrated with a masculine growl as she pushed back, as eager to explore the kiss as he, reveling in her freedom to taste him. Knowing Kade wanted her was heady, a pleasure that mesmerized her, filled an emptiness inside her that had been there as long as she could remember.

Kade. Kade. Kade.

Her hips moved forward, her pussy trying to get closer to his engorged member, cursing the layers of denim between them.

Closer. I need to get closer.

Asha knew she was drowning, losing control, but she gave herself over to Kade without a coherent thought, the needs of her body taking priority. She tore her mouth from his and begged, "Please. Oh, please," she panted, needing more, frantic for more.

Kade lifted her easily onto the kitchen counter, bringing her breasts directly in front of his face. She gasped as he tore off the buttons of her shirt to get it open. Scantily endowed, she had gone braless, and the cool air hitting her sensitive, pebbled nipples was a shock.

"My shirt," she murmured breathlessly, more embarrassed about her small breasts being revealed than the actual clothing.

"I bought you more," Kade growled as his mouth sought and found one breast, his other hand coming up to tease the other.

Asha cradled his head against her breast, still panting with need. "Kade. Please." His fingers and mouth nipped, pinched, and then stroked, driving her need too high, too desperate. Her head fell back against the cupboard, her body feeling like liquid fire as Kade's mouth devoured her breasts, switching from one to the other, as though he wanted to own them both.

She whimpered, her hands on his shoulders to keep herself from crumpling on the counter.

"You're so beautiful, Asha. So sweet I could lick and taste every inch of you and still want more," Kade hissed, his tongue teasing her nipple.

"Small breasts," she said disjointedly, unable to concentrate on anything except Kade's heated torture.

"Perfect," he insisted, his hands cupping her breasts, each thumb teasing a nipple.

Asha squirmed on the counter, the heat and need pulsating between her thighs unbearable. "I need…" she groaned, not quite sure exactly what she needed to make her body stop quivering.

"I know what you need," Kade answered, his voice low and sultry, his heated breath against her neck. "You need a man to make you come. And that man is going to be me."

Asha shuddered as she felt his hand move slowly down her belly, caressing her naked skin as he moved lower and lower. The button on her jeans popped open, the zipper yanked down impatiently, and suddenly, Kade's fingers were there where she needed them, gliding easily through her wet folds and zeroing in on her clit. Each stroke of his talented fingers drew a ragged moan from her lips. She closed her eyes, the pleasure so sharp and intense that it nearly made her come undone. "Yes," she whispered. "Touch me." Opening her thighs wider, she wrapped her legs around Kade's hips, thrusting forward with every stroke of his fingers.

"I don't know if I can take this." Asha's chest was heaving, her entire body quaking with the intensity of her impending climax.

Cupping the back of her head, Kade demanded, "Take it, Asha. Enjoy the ride. Look at me."

Her eyes opened obediently, her whole body going up in flames as her gaze met his, the blue fire shooting from his eyes nearly incinerating her.

"Come for me, sweetheart. You're so wet, so fucking hot. Take what you need and let it all go."

Kade was relentless, his fingers repeatedly stroking over her clit, teasing her into a frenzy of hot, jumbled need. His will was strong, and Asha could feel his determination. In the end, she had very little choice but to let her climax roll over her, unable to hold back her moans and whimpers as it rocked her body helplessly. "Kade," she groaned as she finally closed her eyes, unable to bear the intense look on his handsome face. "Too much."

He kept stroking her as her orgasm subsided, extending it, while his lips captured hers in a kiss, a masculine groan escaping right before he clamped his mouth to hers.

Wrapping her arms around his neck, she kissed him like her life depended on it, savoring the taste of him, wishing she could crawl inside him and never come out again.

Ending the passionate embrace, Kade pulled her shivering body against his and cradled her head against his heaving chest. Both his arms wrapped around her like steel bands, holding her against him like she was someone precious to him. And for just a few moments in time, Asha let herself luxuriate in the feel of his body, revel in the sense of belonging. Trying to turn off her brain that was telling her that what had just happened wasn't right, Asha let her heart lead for once in her life, and wrapped her arms around Kade's ripped, strong body, letting him hold her close. Maybe it was a false sense of protection, but it felt so good that she didn't want it to end.

"Best damn thing in the world," Kade said in a cocky, masculine whisper against her ear.

"What?" she murmured, confused.

"That's how you watch a woman come, sweetheart," Kade answered arrogantly. "And it's fucking fantastic."

Knowing she should probably be mortified because she'd just let a man she barely knew bring her to climax in the middle of the day on a kitchen counter, Asha opened her mouth to chastise him for his arrogance. But then she closed it again, no words spoken. Honestly, she *couldn't* answer. He was right. It had been better than good. Kade had rocked her world, and something told her she'd never be the same again.

Finally, she simply said, "Thank you."

"For what?" Kade asked, confused.

Asha wasn't sure she could really explain, wasn't sure exactly how to express the way she felt. "For making me feel like a desirable woman," she answered simply. How long had she felt broken and defective because her female organs were incapable of producing a child? "I don't feel so damaged anymore."

Kade's arms tightened around her reflexively. "If you think you're damaged, you should see my fucked-up leg," he grumbled.

"You should see my screwed-up lady parts," she retorted lightly, trying to make fun of herself to take Kade's mind off his injury. Honestly, *she'd* never seen her damaged parts. She just knew she was internally flawed.

"If that's an invitation, I'd be more than happy to see them," Kade's sexy baritone voice offered hopefully. "They all felt perfect to me, but I'd love to do a closer examination."

Realizing exactly what she'd said to distract him, Asha laughed delightedly, beginning to feel a feminine power that she'd never experienced before. Her laughter ended in a short cough, a little residual effect of her illness.

"Dammit. I forgot that you're still sick," Kade said as though he were irritated with himself.

"I'm fine," she told him adamantly.

Kade lifted her gently from the counter, letting her slide down his body before she found her feet. "You'll rest before we eat dinner," he replied anxiously, righting her clothes before taking her hand and tugging her gently to lead her out of the kitchen.

Asha barely had time to scoop up her purse and bag before she followed him.

Chapter 5

"I can find a place to stay, Kade. You don't have to put me up while I'm working," Asha said nervously.

The hair at back of Kade's neck stood on end. The thought of Asha wandering around Tampa, looking for a place to stay, while still not fully recovered from her pneumonia, made him want to throw her over his shoulder and deposit her in his bed with him there to watch over her. There was no fucking way she was leaving his house right now. Finding out she had been abused by her asshole of an ex-husband had nearly made him come unglued. "You're staying," he answered simply. "And you're not a damn employee. You're a guest."

Kade passed his own bedroom regrettably, leading her to the room across from his and opening the door. It was only room he'd skipped on their tour. He smiled as he entered, knowing immediately that Mia and Maddie had been here. It was the only room in his entire house liberally splashed with color. "Your room," he told Asha, completely certain he was going to be hard every single night knowing she was sleeping across the hall from him. He was used to her draping her sweet body over his, seeking him out in her sleep. Fuck! He was going to miss that. But he needed to stop pushing her, needed to let her get used to him and his world. Stubbornly, he wanted her to come to him, want him. Having her here would be both heaven and hell, but after finding out about her abuse, he needed to stifle his caveman instincts.

Her mouth dropped open as she moved slowly forward, her eyes darting around the room. "It's beautiful," she said reverently as her hand smoothed over the colorful quilt on the king-sized bed.

Mia and Maddie had outdone themselves. Bright pictures and wall-hangings decorated the walls, and the quilt she was stroking had every color of the rainbow bursting from the material. Kade opened the closet, already knowing what he would find. He'd asked Mia and Maddie to fix up his guest room and make it as happy and colorful as possible. Giving them Asha's size from her spare clothing, he'd also requested that they stock her some clothes. Judging by the full closet, they'd taken his request seriously. "Mia and Maddie got you some clothes."

Asha turned and looked at the closet, coming up beside him to finger the materials. "Which ones?" she asked cautiously.

"All of them are yours. I let my sister and Maddie pick them out. I just told them you like colorful things."

"Why would they do this?" Asha said uncomfortably, holding her buttonless shirt closed with her hand.

"I've seen them. I've played with them. I've had my mouth on them, which was one of the most amazing moments of my life. You don't have to hide your breasts from me," he told her, amused.

Asha's face flushed from his comment, but she didn't acknowledge it. "I can't accept these. Every one of these is designer labeled. My whole wardrobe has never been worth what one single shirt in this collection costs," Asha told him adamantly, looking up at him with a frown. "Why would someone I don't know buy me clothes?"

Her brow crinkled when she was upset, making Kade want to smooth it out with his fingers and lips. "Because I asked them to do it and they wanted to do it. You don't like the outfits?"

"They're beautiful, but I can't accept. You've done far too much for me, and you already gave me gifts."

"Yeah, you can. They were a gift from your sister. And there isn't a limit on giving gifts." The stubborn woman needed clothes, and she was taking them.

"I don't have a sister," Asha answered warily.

"You do have a sister and a brother. And these are just clothes. It's not a big deal. If it makes you feel any better, Maddie married one of the richest men in the world, Sam Hudson. She wanted to do this for you." Kade knew Asha already knew the details about her probable siblings, but she obviously wasn't ready to accept the reality. He didn't have a doubt in his mind that she was related to Max and Maddie. Her mother had the same maiden name, and Asha had showed him a photo of her mother with her natural father, a picture that showed an older, but very similar, version of the photo that Max had of his natural mother, Alice. "Why is it so hard to accept that Max and Maddie are your sister and brother? I know it's a shock. Maddie was surprised to find Max. But she was happy."

Asha's eyes started to water, and she turned her back on him and sat gingerly on the bed. "I've never had family. My foster parents fed me and clothed me, but I was never really one of them. They took me in before they had two children of their own. I never really belonged, and I felt the distance. It's hard to explain without sounding like I'm feeling sorry for myself. I'm grateful to them. But I was never really part of the family." Tears flowed down her cheeks, her eyes guarded. "I'm afraid, scared to believe in something that might not be true. What if I love them and they don't love me back? What if I'm not really their sister?"

Kade's chest tightened as he looked at Asha, small and vulnerable, yet strong enough to walk away from a relationship with nothing in order to save herself and her sanity. Had anyone ever cared about her unconditionally, just because she was an incredible woman? "You *are* their sister. And they'll love you back." How could they not? "Trust me," he asked her huskily, knowing trust probably wouldn't come easy for her, but he wanted it pretty damn desperately. In fact, he was beginning to covet it more than anything else he'd ever wanted.

Asha crossed her legs on the bed, her bare feet peeking out from under her jean-clad legs. She looked up at him wistfully. "Even if we are related, we're so different. They're incredibly wealthy and I'm used to being poor. They're American and I'm Indian—"

"You're American, too," Kade growled, annoyed that Asha saw herself as "less than" compared to her siblings. "And even if you weren't, it wouldn't matter."

"We were raised in different cultures. And they both look like our mother," Asha answered quietly.

"Maddie was a foster child, passed around from family to family, none of them giving a shit about her. She worked her ass off to get through medical school, and she had no family either until Max found her." Kade sat down on the bed and pulled Asha into his lap. "She's excited about having a sister. And so is Max."

"Poor Maddie," Asha whispered sympathetically. "Is she really happy now? Is Max?"

Kade's lips turned up in a small smile as he looked at Asha's troubled expression, touched by how quickly Asha could feel remorse about Maddie's earlier circumstances. She had a huge heart, just like Maddie. She was more like her sister than she knew. He'd told her everything about Max and Mia's life, including the torture Max had suffered when Mia had disappeared for two years and was assumed dead. He'd seen the same sweet concern when he'd told her about that horrible time in all their lives.

"They're both ecstatically happy," Kade assured her, stroking the silky hair from Asha's face. "They each married their soul mate. But neither one of them exactly had it easy. And they aren't so different from you. Their difficulties were just different. They never really had family either, Asha. Give them a chance."

Give me a chance, too.

Kade knew he was far from being emotionally healthy, but damned if he didn't feel like being with Asha was healing some of his emotional wounds from his past.

She's mine.

"Do you believe in soul mates, relationships like Maddie and Max have with Mia and Sam? Do you believe there's one person in every life made just for you?" Asha asked softly.

A few weeks ago, Kade would have answered with a resounding *"hell no."* He'd always been the first one to give Max and Sam hell for being so nauseatingly sappy about their wives. Now, he just didn't know. He'd been mysteriously drawn to Asha even before he'd met her, through their game of cat and mouse, and then through her drawings. She was like a balm to his battered soul, a remedy for his loneliness. He'd never felt like that about a woman before, and it confounded him. "Yeah. Yeah, I think I do," he answered as he looked down into her eyes, losing himself in the swirling, molten brown of her gaze. Every cell in his body was calling out for him to claim her as his, and he had to clench his fists behind her back and in her hair to keep from stripping her naked and showing her what it was like to be really wanted by a man so desperately that he had to have her. He wanted to show her what it was like to be respected and cherished.

He didn't care if she was related to Maddie and Max.

And he couldn't care less if she couldn't conceive a child.

He just wanted…her. And he wanted to stake his claim on her so badly that his big body shuddered with need.

"I think so, too. But what happens if you never find that person?" she asked thoughtfully.

You've found him. You don't need to keep looking. You belong with me.

"I think it just happens," he answered aloud. "If you're destined to be together, you find each other somehow."

"My foster mother always told me I was too fanciful. My drawings, my reading, my mind always everywhere except on the practical things in life," Asha said with a sigh. "I guess in some ways, I didn't completely conform to being the practical Indian woman they wanted."

"You don't need to conform. You come from an Indian heritage, and you can be proud of that. Many Indians are kind people.

But you're also American. And the majority of American women don't put up with a whole lot of shit." He lay back on the bed and stretched out his legs, his right calf starting to ache. Catching her around the waist, he pulled her down against him, resting her head on his chest.

Her head popped back up and she looked at him excitedly. "Have you been to India?"

He nodded. "Several times. Harrison Corporation has business interests there."

"What's it like?" she asked wistfully. "Isn't it strange that I was raised in the Indian culture, but I've never been there?"

"I'll take you there one day. At least you can probably speak the language," he answered jokingly.

"Only if we go to Andhra Pradesh or an area that speaks Telugu," she answered thoughtfully. "My foster parents and ex-husband were all from there and spoke Telugu. I never learned much Hindi."

"It always amazes me that two Indians can't necessarily speak to each other because there are so many languages in India," Kade answered.

Asha laid her head back down on Kade's chest and started to fiddle with the buttons on his red shirt that was decorated with dancing banana characters. "I know women get beaten there too," she said hesitantly. "I've been reading a lot about India when I get the chance. The domestic violence there is pretty bad. It's almost as if it's acceptable. Are most women treated badly there?"

"Hitting a woman is never acceptable for any reason," Kade grumbled. "Men who beat women, American or Indian, are fucking cowards, too afraid to pick a fight with someone who might actually win and mess them up." He sighed as he continued, "I wish I could tell you that things are great, but the domestic violence rate in India is high. I was there on business, and I never was totally immersed in the culture, but it's still a patriarchal society and there's a large percentage of men there who don't value their women the way they should. And equal opportunity is definitely not there, even though there are laws to protect women now. They're just basically not enforced. The younger generation is trying to bring about change, but it's an uphill battle."

"And divorce is still taboo," she added wistfully.

Kade couldn't lie. "For the most part...yeah. It's not widely acceptable. But you aren't in India, Asha." Trying to change the subject, he asked curiously, "You've never told me why you still use your father's last name? If you were married, didn't you take on his last name?"

"My married name was Kota, but I took my father's name back when I divorced Ravi. I guess it was my way of taking control of my own identity again."

Kade actually liked the fact that she had taken her father's name back and no longer carried the name of an asshole. "Will the butterfly ever escape from the cocoon?" he asked distractedly, his hand toying with the silky strands of her hair.

Her head came up and she gave him a shy grin. "It's a process. Every time I feel like I'm progressing, I'll make the wings emerge a little further."

Kade felt his heart lighten at the sight of her smile. He decided that he wanted to see that happy expression on her face constantly, every hour, every minute of every day. She'd seen enough pain and conflict in her twenty-seven years of life. Asha was born to shine, and Kade wanted to make everything easier for her after the fucked-up deal she'd had. "When do you think that might happen?"

She grinned broader. "After that experience on the kitchen counter, I think I at least need to poke another tiny bit of the wing from the cocoon."

Kade groaned inwardly, his swollen cock twitching with the desire to do some poking of its own. Her smile made his heart swell, and the fact that she was comfortable enough with him to mention that earth-shattering, intimate experience now without hesitation made him feel like they were caught up in their own little world.

She belongs with me.

Kade couldn't stop the possessive, animalistic need to conquer her, to hold her so close she'd never go away. If she did, the light that she'd turned on inside him would die. Something was happening to him, something incredible. And he didn't want the exhilarating feeling to end. Bit by bit, the darkness inside him was being chased away by Asha's glowing presence.

With a mock growl, he flipped her over, pinning her body beneath his, and it felt fucking fantastic. Holding her arms captive over her head, he felt carnal satisfaction at having her exactly where he wanted her. "I'd be more than happy to go for making the butterfly emerge completely." In fact, he was fairly certain he was going to go insane if he didn't get inside her very soon. He wanted the damned butterfly spreading its wings to hurry up and fly.

Kade felt her body tremble beneath him, her expression part longing and part trepidation. He knew he was pushing her too hard, too fast, but he couldn't seem to control the urge to take her. Watching her, and feeling her climax beneath his fingers had been incredible, but he wanted to give her more, show her that a woman's pleasure could be much more than tolerable. And selfishly, he just wanted her to want him.

Gritting his teeth with the pain of wanting to fuck her until she was screaming his name, he watched her face, waiting for a sign—any damn sign—that she wanted the same thing he did, felt the same way he was feeling.

"I'm here to do a job," she said brokenly. "I can't do this."

"Fuck the job. This is about you and me. It's never been about the job. You're incredibly talented, and I wish you'd do your magic on every damn wall in this house, but it isn't why I wanted you here," he admitted, frustrated.

"You brought me here because of your sister and Max?" she asked, her voice resigned.

"I brought you here because I couldn't let you go. It's pretty simple. I just want you," he said hoarsely, knowing he was giving her enough rope to hang him, but he didn't give a shit. For once, control and keeping his emotions in check didn't mean a goddamn thing to him. "I want to breathe in your scent, and I swear, from this day forward, the smell of jasmine will always make my cock hard enough to pound nails. I want to taste your orgasm on my tongue, make you come until you can't think about anything but me. And I need to be inside you, fucking you until you don't even know your own name." Kade swallowed hard, and added, "Then I want you to sleep with me, and I want to keep you so close that you'll never know another moment of wondering if anybody wants you—because I do, Asha. I want you enough to make up for every person in your life who didn't."

She looked at him, her open-mouthed expression completely stunned. "I'm nobody special. I don't understand."

Kade dropped his head to her shoulder with a groan, knowing he'd made a complete ass out of himself. "You are special. That's what I'm trying to tell you."

She yanked at her wrists, and Kade released her reluctantly. His mind and body were screaming at him to keep her, but she obviously didn't understand how he felt. Hell, he didn't even understand it himself. His feelings for her were out-of-control crazy, but he couldn't help being a lunatic. His emotions were stronger than his common sense.

Expecting her to push him off her, Kade shuddered as he felt her hands hesitantly push underneath his shirt and up his back, exploring and wandering across his bare skin. Her lips against his ear, she whispered, "I'm homeless and barely surviving. My boobs are too small, and I'm no seductress. I've only been with one man in my entire life, and sex was never something I really wanted or thought I needed. But I'm starting to crave you, and it scares me. I don't know why you want me, but I can guarantee I want you more. I know I shouldn't be telling you how I feel, but I can't let you think I don't want you back. Because I do. I want you so much it hurts."

Kade lifted his head, his expression incredulous as he started to drown in her swirling chocolate eyes. Her words made him come completely unraveled, but he needed her to understand that he wanted more than a fuck. "I don't care where you come from, or how much money you do or don't have. I just want to be with you because of who you are. You're brave, talented, smart, sexy and completely insane to want a lame, washed-up jock like me, but I'm glad you do," he answered in a shaky, low voice, his emotions out of control. Asha had tapped into his hidden emotional well, and he was tangled in a web of need so tightly that he couldn't extricate himself, and he wasn't sure he wanted to escape.

"Stop it." Asha speared her hands into his hair and pulled his face close to hers. "You're the kindest man I've ever met, you're incredibly handsome and sexy, and I couldn't care less if you can't play football anymore. And I think your ex-girlfriend was either crazy or incredibly superficial if she couldn't see what she had. I want you because of who you are, too. I don't even understand football. It's just a silly game."

"Whoa! Hold on. Don't call football silly," he scolded her in a teasing voice, resting his forehead against hers. "It was my entire life for years."

"Maybe it's time to make a new life," Asha suggested hesitantly. "You have so much more to offer the world than just playing a game. I know how much it meant to you. It would be like taking away my ability to do my art. But you're more than just one thing, Kade."

He swallowed hard, moved by her faith in him. Yeah. Maybe it was time to start a new chapter in his life, just like Asha was trying to do for herself. And he could think of nothing better than beginning it with the woman beneath him. He could happily drown in her seductive scent, bury himself inside her until he didn't give a shit about anything else but her. And he'd quite gladly take on the task of making her happy and keeping her that way. "Maybe it is time to do something else," he agreed in a graveled voice, moving the few inches needed to cover her tempting, lush lips with his own.

Her instant response just fueled the flames that were already consuming him. She met his tongue stroke for stroke, squirming beneath him to unbutton his shirt. Finally, he felt the buttons pop, and his shirt parted, their bare skin finally meeting. And Kade completely lost it. The feel of her naked breasts—that he personally found to be the perfect size—sliding against his chest felt so incredibly erotic that he was desperate to get her naked, to feel their entire bodies skin-to-skin.

"Touch me," he demanded as he pulled his mouth from hers. He needed her hands on his heated skin before he went completely insane. Her fingers had just started their shy exploration, were almost to the waistband of his jeans, when Kade heard a noise from downstairs.

"Kade? Are you here?" The voice was coming from the kitchen and it was definitely female.

"Fuck!" His sister had shitty timing. And he should have known he wouldn't have to let her know he was home. No doubt Mia passed by his house on a daily basis, waiting. Kade wanted to lock the bedroom door and ignore it, but he knew he couldn't, even though he was pretty sure his balls were as blue as a Smurf.

Asha froze beneath him, her expression startled. "Who is it?"

Kade clenched his jaw tightly and forced himself to move from the sweet haven between Asha's jean-clad thighs. "It's Mia—your new pain-in-the-ass sister-in-law." Kade loved his sister, but considering what she'd interrupted, he wanted nothing more than for her to go away for at least a week. Or maybe two. "No doubt Maddie is with her, and probably Max."

Kade stood and Asha scrambled to her feet, holding her buttonless shirt in front of her. "Oh, God. I'm not ready for this," she groaned.

He grinned at her wickedly. "I guess you better find a shirt."

Watching her scurry around the room, pulling open drawers frantically, made him smile even wider. She looked so adorable when she was frazzled. Rifling through her bag, she pulled out a bra, jerked it on and snapped it in the front. Kade scowled, thinking *that* was a real pity.

"Can you grab me a shirt?" she asked nervously, looking in the mirror and frowning at her reflection. "I look like I just tumbled out of bed," she said, her voice tremulous.

"You did," he answered, sounding pleased with himself. Knowing it was his fault that she was somewhat tousled made him want to take her back to bed and finish the job.

"I don't want them to know that," she hissed, pulling a brush from her purse and yanking it mercilessly through her long hair.

"Kade?" Mia's voice sounded again, closer this time.

He strode to the bedroom door and yelled, "We'll be down in a minute." The last thing he wanted was to be confronted by Mia, Max, and Maddie in Asha's bedroom. Their appearance would lead to questions he couldn't or didn't want to answer. He supposed he should get another shirt for himself, but he strolled to the closet and browsed the selection Mia had picked for Asha. Pulling out a bright red silk with a swirling black design, he pulled it from the hanger and walked over to Asha. He held the shirt open while she slipped her arms into the sleeves and hastily buttoned the front. He took the brush from her hand and set it on the dresser. "Stop torturing your hair. You look beautiful," he told her gruffly, taking her hand and leading her across the hall.

He grabbed another shirt from his bedroom closet and shrugged it on before reaching for her hand again. "Ready?"

"No. I'm a coward. I don't want to go down there," she told him honestly, her voice panicked.

"Then don't," he told her simply. "I'll go down and make something up. If you're not ready to meet them, they can wait."

Asha sighed. "I can't do that to them. They've been nice enough to come meet me. I can't be rude. I don't want to hurt their feelings."

Kade shrugged. "Sure you can. If you're not ready, then they can wait." Really, his main concern was whether or not Asha was comfortable. Maddie, Mia, and Max were here because they couldn't contain their curiosity; Asha was scared shitless.

"I'm fine," she murmured, tightening her hold on his hand.

Asha was clinging to him, but he had no complaints. She could lean on him all she wanted. He'd be there for her anytime she needed him. That was another thing he couldn't explain—he actually *wanted* her to need him, to be able to count on him to have her back in any bad situation.

Shaking his head at his thoughts, he let go of her hand and wrapped an arm around her waist, bringing her body tightly against his in a protective gesture.

They left the room silently, but Kade never let her go, even after they arrived downstairs.

Chapter 6

Asha tried really hard not to feel inferior to the women waiting in Kade's living room, but failed miserably. Amid the introductions, she tried to wrap her mind around the fact that she could actually be related to these sophisticated, wealthy people. *Not possible.* They were nothing alike. She couldn't quite believe that the handsome, dark-haired Max who had his arm wrapped around Mia could be her brother. Or that the lovely red-headed physician who introduced herself as Maddie could be her sister. These people were completely out of her league, and she inwardly cringed at what they might be thinking about *her.*

Her hair needed a more thorough brushing, her jeans were tattered, and her feet were bare, the henna tattoo on her foot peeking out from under the denim of her jeans. The only nice thing she was wearing was the beautiful red blouse, and *that* had been provided by the two women in front of her. God...she was a mess. Even if she *was* related to them, they certainly wouldn't want to claim *her.*

"You can come and stay with us," Mia said cheerfully, after everyone was introduced.

"No. I want her to stay with Sam and me," Maddie said emphatically.

Asha heard a low growling noise coming from Kade. "She's staying here," he rumbled, glaring at all of his guests. "She's doing some designs for me."

"What kind of designs?" Mia asked curiously.

"I do wall designs," Asha answered quietly, suddenly wishing she had a more stable career, more education, or anything that would make her feel less like a loser next to these people.

"She's an incredible artist," Kade boasted proudly, his arm tightening around Asha's waist.

Mia smiled at her before answering, "I design jewelry. I'd love to see your work."

"I have some pictures upstairs," Asha answered hesitantly, fairly certain Mia was just being polite. No doubt Mia had been to college, studied her craft. Asha was self-taught, using her gut instinct and raw talent to create her designs.

Mia's expression lit up. "Let's go look," she said excitedly, Maddie's head bobbing in agreement.

"Hold it," Max boomed as the two women pulled her from Kade's reassuring grasp. "I'd like to hug my sister first before you drag her off for a female bonding session."

Asha stepped back, her whole body trembling, desperately wanting the brotherly affection that Max was offering, but terrified to accept it. She had no time to think before Max moved forward and pulled her into his arms, wrapping her into a bear hug. Strangely, there was nothing awkward about Max's embrace, and although it was a little disconcerting for her because she wasn't used to physical affection, she felt a sense of peace and security when he held her against his strong body. She felt nothing but acceptance vibrating from his strong frame, and tears sprang to her eyes as she hesitantly hugged him back. "I'm not used to having anyone," she whispered huskily without thinking about her words.

Max hugged her even tighter and said, "You have us. I'm sorry it took so long to find you." He eased up and held her by the shoulders. "I know this is overwhelming. I didn't have family either until I found Maddie. Finding you is an enormous gift to both Maddie and me."

"I was alone, too," Maddie said, as she pulled Asha away from Max and hugged her almost as tightly as her brother had.

Asha felt the same sense of connection as Maddie hugged her close, and the tears streamed from her eyes like a river. These two people were so willing to accept her as a sister, to pull her into the fold of their family. It was overwhelming and wonderful, but frightening. While she hungered for family, wanted it with every cell in her body, the unknowns of the situation were also terrifying. She'd always been alone. What did she know about a real family?

Finally, she pulled away from Maddie, swiping at her tears with her hand. "We can't be certain I'm really related." She reminded herself of the reality that nothing was completely proven. It wouldn't do to get attached to the idea of family and then have it all taken away. It was a seductive lure that she couldn't let take her away from reality.

"I don't need proof," Max said hoarsely. "I can sense it."

"Me too," Maddie agreed. "It's the same strange feeling of being connected that I felt with Max before I knew he and I were siblings. And we know we had the same mother. Her name was the same, and Max's investigation is pretty conclusive since Kade was able to provide more information. We all share the same mother."

"But what if it's all a mistake? What if she just happened to have the same name or something?" Every part of her wanted to believe she had these two extraordinary people for a brother and sister, but it was so surreal that she just couldn't believe it. Things like this didn't happen to her.

Max dug out his wallet and pulled out a picture. "Here. This is our mother. She was very young at the time. It's the only picture I could locate."

Asha took the small picture from him, her heart racing with fear and anticipation. She studied it, biting her lower lip in concentration as she looked at the likeness, a woman who looked very much like Maddie—and a younger version of her own birth mother. Stroking a finger along the edge of the small picture, she murmured, "She does look like my mom."

"Do you have a picture?" Maddie asked excitedly. "I'd like to see it."

"I do. I have a picture of her and my father before they died." Asha handed the picture back to Max.

"Do you remember them?" Max asked, placing the photo back in his wallet. "I know they died in a car accident. Your father was drinking and driving, according to my information."

"Your information was wrong," Asha answered defensively. "My father wasn't driving and he didn't drink. There was no alcohol in his system. But the guy driving was intoxicated. They had all gone together to a holiday party for his work. My mom and dad were in the back seat, and everyone in the car died instantly when the driver swerved and they were hit by a semi-truck." Taking a deep breath, she continued, "And no...I don't remember them. I was only three when they died. I don't have much left from either of them. Once their estate was settled, there was nothing but a few personal belongings." Actually, she had gotten quite a few of her parents' belongings, but everything had been sold off by her foster parents, supposedly to pay for her expenses, leaving her with nothing but a few photos.

Maddie put her arm around her, as though she sensed Asha's sadness. "Let's go look at those pictures."

"I'm sorry, Asha," Max said remorsefully. "No child should have to lose both of her parents so young."

Asha shrugged. "We all did." She knew Max had been adopted by good parents, but Maddie had done the rounds of foster homes and knew what it was like to feel alone.

"I was luckier than you and Maddie," Max answered contritely.

She looked up at Max, and wanted to hug him again when she saw his rueful expression. "I'm glad at least one of us got adopted. It's not your fault that I didn't. I survived. I had foster parents who fed me and gave me a roof over my head."

Maddie chuckled. "Don't bother trying to tell him that. You'll soon learn that Max feels like a brother who should have been there for his sisters, even though he didn't even know we existed. Maybe together we can convince him that he's not psychic and isn't responsible for our problems."

Asha smiled shyly at Maddie. "Things happen. It's nobody's fault." Shooting Max a warm smile, she let Maddie and Mia lead her toward the stairs.

"We'll throw something on the grill. I'm starving," Kade grumbled. "Don't be gone long."

After the three women climbed the stairs and entered Asha's temporary bedroom, she looked at Mia and Maddie and said, "They're actually going to cook?" She'd never once seen her foster father cook, and her ex-husband certainly hadn't.

Mia and Maddie both flopped on Asha's bed, making themselves comfortable. "Kade is a little scary in the culinary department, but Max is a decent cook. And Maddie's husband, Sam, almost always cooks. He makes some incredible food," Mia answered, folding her legs beneath her on the bed and looking at Asha with a perplexed look. "You look surprised."

"I've never seen a husband who actually cooked," she answered, still surprised that Maddie's billionaire husband actually spent time in the kitchen.

"Sam hasn't let me fix a meal since I got pregnant," Maddie said with a sigh. "He's a little freaked out that I'm having twins. Kade told us that you were married for seven years. Don't tell me that your ex-husband never made a meal."

Asha shook her head. "Never. My foster parents were very conservative Indians and so was my ex-husband. Men don't cook." She watched Maddie as she stretched out on the bed, noticing for the first time that her new sister had a baby bump. She hadn't seen it beneath the flowing shirt Maddie was wearing, but it was pretty recognizable now that she was lying on the bed with the material stretched over her distended belly. "You're having twins?" she asked, her tone slightly awed.

Maddie smiled dreamily. "Yes. Much to my husband's dismay. He's thrilled, but he worries about the risk factors."

Mia snorted. "If your man never cooked, I'm surprised you lasted seven years with him."

"It was the acceptable thing in my culture. My foster parents were very traditional immigrants and so was my ex-husband. They were used to the woman doing the cooking, cleaning, and female chores."

"Maybe it's time to learn more about your American culture," Maddie mused. "Most women work or take care of children, and men share responsibilities. If they don't, we give them a swift kick in the ass."

Asha smiled at Maddie's comment as she dug into her purse, looking for her photos, and continued to explain what her life had been like to Maddie and Mia because they asked what seemed like a million questions about her upbringing and her marriage. She answered all their questions, skirting around the domestic abuse part of her history. Finally, she found the photo of her mother and father, along with her pictures of her work.

"So they sold you?" Maddie said angrily, sounding as outraged as Kade, virtually repeating his words, after Asha told the two women vaguely about her marriage, minus the abuse details. "Honey, it wasn't all about the culture. There are Indian women here who are doctors, lawyers, and rocket scientists. You're American with Indian blood, but you're still American and living in America. And Indian women do incredible things here, get wonderful educations. I think your foster family and your ex-husband thought they were still living in India. And I don't think they were very nice people either, regardless of their heritage."

Asha sighed and plopped into a chair beside the bed. "My foster parents don't talk to me anymore because I divorced Ravi." Not that they had communicated with her much anyway after her marriage. They spoke to Ravi, but they rarely asked about her.

"We get to screen your next husband," Mia said, her voice making the statement sound more like a threat than a joke. "If there's no give-and-take in the relationship, you can't marry him."

"I won't marry again," Asha answered in a hushed voice.

"Of course you will. Mia and I were both older than you when we married Max and Sam," Maddie said fiercely. "You just need the right guy this time."

"I can't have children," Asha admitted reluctantly. For some reason, these two women made her want to spill all her secrets to them.

"You can adopt if you want kids. And depending on the reason, there could be other options. Do you know why you can't conceive?" Maddie asked gently.

"I don't know. It didn't really matter. Ravi said he got checked and he was fine. He said it was my defect."

"You're not defective just because you can't have a child," Maddie said, exasperated. "Marry a man you love, and you can work out the rest when the time comes. Love is everything, Asha. You can work around other problems."

Asha fidgeted uncomfortably in her chair. "There was never love in my marriage."

"There will be next time," Mia said sympathetically. "Maddie and I will make sure of it."

Asha didn't think there would be a next time for her, but she smiled at the two women on the bed, her heart squeezing inside her chest because they were concerned about *her*.

This is what it's like to have friends. Real friends who care.

"Thanks," she said simply, handing Maddie the photo of her parents, and Mia her work pictures.

"Your father was very handsome. And this is definitely our mother," Maddie mused, staring at the photo Asha had handed her. "She looks happy."

"I like to think they were very happy," Asha told Maddie.

Maddie leaned back on the bed, stretching her back. "She had a difficult life. I hope she was happy in the end."

"You're not bitter about her giving you and Max up?" Asha questioned, wondering how Maddie could sound so sincere about wishing her mother happiness.

"No. Not anymore. I have Sam, and I'm happier than I could ever have dreamed I would be. Whatever happened, I like to think she did it to give Max and me a better life. Maybe she had no choice." Her hand went protectively to her belly, rubbing it absently. "How my life is now makes up for any unhappiness I had in my earlier life. We're having babies, and I have a brother and sister now. I don't have any regrets. I have a wonderful future to look forward to. Everything that happened has led me to this wonderful life and Sam."

Maddie was glowing, and Asha knew it wasn't just from the pregnancy. *That* was the look of supreme happiness, and Mia had the same glow. Did loving a good man really make a woman this happy? Sadly, Asha was fairly certain she'd never know.

"These are really fantastic," Mia squealed, flipping through the photos of Asha's work.

Maddie leaned over to look at the photos with Mia, their heads close together while they perused the pictures. "No wonder Kade wants you to put some life into this house. Your designs will add a lot of warmth to this place."

Asha smiled as the two women eagerly tried to wheedle an appointment for themselves. Maddie wanted her nursery done, and Mia wanted her workshop wall decorated, saying she'd love the inspiration. She wondered if they really meant it, or if they were just being polite. Still, she was happily flustered that they seemed to like her work.

"Food's done," Kade yelled impatiently from the bottom of the stairs.

The women rose to their feet. Mia went ahead, as though she were already eager to see her husband's face again. Maddie lingered, handing Asha back her picture of her parents. She gathered the pictures of her work that Mia had left on the dresser and put them all back in her bag.

"Asha...are you really okay staying with Kade?" Maddie asked, concerned. "I want you with me and my home is always open if you want to stay with Sam and me. You need some time to get on your feet after your divorce."

"Do you think it's inappropriate for me to stay with him?" Asha asked hesitantly. She was a single woman. Kade was a single man. Maybe it wasn't such a good idea. But the thought of leaving Kade right now wasn't a comfortable one. He'd taken care of her while she was sick, and although he unsettled her at times, she liked being near him. And she trusted him.

"Of course it's not inappropriate. You're both single adults. I just want to make sure you're comfortable. I saw the way Kade was looking at you. I think he's already getting…uh…attached." Maddie looked like she wanted to say something else, but she looked at Asha solemnly.

"I'm fine here," she answered, relieved that she wouldn't have to leave Kade so soon. "And he's just being…nice."

"Bullshit. Kade's protective of you, possessive. I think he's been bitten by the caveman bug," Maddie said emphatically.

"Caveman bug?" Asha answered in a confused tone.

Maddie grimaced. "The alpha-male-pounding-on-his-chest syndrome. He's starting to care about you, Asha."

Lowering her head, she replied weakly, "Don't worry. I won't get attached to him. I know he's way out of my league."

Maddie grasped her shoulders and shook her lightly. "Nobody is out of your league. I'm just warning you that he's not just being nice. Believe me, I know the Tarzan look starting to emerge. I have to admit that it surprised me. I've never seen this side of Kade."

Asha looked into Maddie's hazel eyes, and saw that they were warm with affection. She swallowed hard and answered honestly, "Maddie…I'm homeless, I'm poor, and I never even went to college. What use would Kade Harrison have for me other than to paint his walls?" Okay, maybe he wanted to have sex with her, but Asha didn't think there was anything more to his attention than that. Not really.

"I was poor when I met Sam again. I was deep into student loans, and I didn't have a penny to spare because I wanted to run a free clinic. None of that matters if you're supposed to be together. You're talented and brave; you're a survivor. Don't ever think you're not good enough." Maddie let her hands drop to her side and raised a brow at Asha. "You like him."

"Who wouldn't?" Asha said, giving Maddie a small smile. "He's handsome, smart, sweet, and he wears gorgeous shirts."

"Oh, God. You like his shirts? That's not good," Maddie mumbled.

"What was his girlfriend like? I think she hurt him," Asha asked, unable to stop herself.

"She was a grade A bitch," Maddie answered angrily. "When Kade was a star quarterback, he was larger than life. Sam says he was one of the best quarterbacks of our generation. He could have had any woman that he wanted, but he stayed faithful for years to a woman who didn't want anything except his celebrity status to enhance her modeling career. She dumped him in a hurry when he couldn't help her visibility in fashionable circles anymore. He's a good man. I don't think any of us ever understood why he stayed with her. Maybe it was habit, or maybe he didn't know anything else. Losing his career and getting dumped because he wasn't perfect anymore probably did a number on his self-esteem. He already came from the same screwed-up background that Mia did. He didn't deserve what happened to him."

"Was his childhood bad?" Asha asked tentatively, knowing it was none of her business, but still wanting to know. Kade didn't talk about his childhood. He spoke about his family, but most of the events he shared were recent.

Maddie snorted. "Bad? His childhood makes ours look like paradise. His father was a mental case who drank. Kade, Mia, and Travis were all pretty badly abused. Then one day, his father killed their mother and then shot himself. It was a major scandal and a stigma that still comes up now and then. It's been a hard incident to shake for all of them."

Asha's chest ached, almost as if she were able to feel the pain of Kade's past. There was silence as a speaking glance passed between her and Maddie, a moment of silent communication where each knew what the other was thinking: Life wasn't fair, and sometimes really bad things happened to good people.

Finally, Asha said timidly, "Maddie?"

"Yeah?" Maddie answered, looking questioningly at Asha.

"I still think Kade's a wonderful man. His leg doesn't matter. I hate that he isn't doing what he loves and I'm sorry his leg causes him some pain. But he's still the same man, and he's splendid." Asha sighed.

Maddie put her hands on her hips and shot Asha an amused look. "You do like him. But remember, he's a man, so it's impossible for him to be perfect."

"Don't you think Sam's perfect?"

"Oh, God, no! He's arrogant, bossy, and way overprotective. And I remind him of that frequently," Maddie answered with laughter in her voice. "But he's also the man who stole my heart and wouldn't give it back. My soul mate. He's kind, loving, and there's nothing he wouldn't do to make me happy. And vice versa. So nope...he's not perfect, but he's perfect for me."

Asha watched Maddie's dreamy eyes and lovesick expression, happy that Maddie finally had the man of her dreams. "I'd like to meet him someday."

"You will. Soon," Maddie promised. "He's anxious to meet you, too. But he was afraid you'd be a little overwhelmed. Sam's brother is married to my best friend, and Simon and Kara would like to meet you, too, when you're feeling more comfortable."

"Hey...where are you two? We're eating," Max bellowed from downstairs.

Maddie and Asha looked at each other and giggled. Max sounded like an angry bear ready to pounce on his food.

"You okay?" Maddie asked, putting her arm around Asha's shoulders. "I know this is all really new for you, and probably confusing."

"I'm good," Asha answered honestly. "I'm actually looking forward to doing some of the walls in this house. I think I'm still having a little culture conflict, caught between the way I was raised and what I really want. I want to be independent and strong, but I'm fighting my past baggage."

"Everything will be okay, Asha. I promise. We're all here to help you get whatever you want."

Unfortunately, Asha wasn't sure it was a case of "whatever she wanted" and not "who she wanted" but she wasn't about to mention that to Maddie. She still had a long way to go before that butterfly was going to emerge and be liberated.

The two of them walked slowly toward the top of the stairs, Asha gently grabbing Maddie's arm before she descended the stairs. "Is there any way we can find out for sure that there's no mistake, that we're really sisters?"

Maddie's brows drew together as she searched Asha's face. "I know you're my sister."

"I want to know for sure. Can we do it?" If anyone would know, it was Maddie. She was a doctor, and if there was a way to see scientific proof, Maddie would know.

"We can do mitochondrial DNA testing since we're just trying to see if we all have the same mother, but we already know we do," Maddie said, her tone puzzled. "I don't need any more proof, Asha. I feel it the same as Max does, and we have plenty of proof."

"I guess it's hard for me to believe," Asha said, shaking her head.

Maddie smoothed back Asha's black hair, placing an errant lock gently behind her ear. "We can do the test. I already know what the results will be because I feel it. I hope someday you'll feel it, too."

Asha did feel it, but she was afraid to believe anything she couldn't prove with scientific evidence. She wanted to tell Maddie that she already felt like her sister, that the bond was already there. But the uncertainty was still there, and she hated it. Why couldn't she believe her gut instinct? Maybe because she'd never listened to it before?

"It's no big deal. We'll do the test," Maddie told her gently, starting down the stairs with her arm around Asha's shoulders. "Have Kade bring you to the clinic and we'll take care of it."

"I know it's stupid to ask for it—"

"No, it's not," Maddie scolded. "Never feel stupid for asking for something you want. You have the right to your own feelings. And don't ever let anyone tell you otherwise."

Asha smiled at Maddie's maternal tone, knowing immediately that her sister was going to make a great mom. Her kids would be strong, brave…and secure. "I'll try to remember that," she answered, her lips curving upward.

"Make sure you do," Maddie replied, hugging Asha tightly when they got to the bottom of the stairs. "We'll do the test, but you *are* my sister, so you better get used to my unsolicited sisterly advice."

The two women smiled at each other, the bond between them growing even stronger, clicking securely in place.

"It's about damn time," Max grumbled as he came out of the dining room and wrapped an arm around both of his sisters. "I was about to waste away from starvation," he continued melodramatically.

"I see you managed to stay alive," Maddie said drily as she wrapped her arm around Max's waist. "You could have gone ahead without us."

"No appreciation for the way Kade and I slaved away in the kitchen," he grumbled goodheartedly.

Asha's heart was light as she continued to watch the sibling banter between Max and Maddie. Her arm slowly crept around Max's waist silently, starting to feel like she was part of the family bond.

"Are you going to be unappreciative, too, Asha?" Max questioned, smiling down at Asha as all three of them walked toward the dining room.

Asha relished his teasing. It was something she'd never had or done before. "It depends on how good the dinner is," she answered cheekily, trying out her bantering skills for the first time.

"Great. Now I'm really screwed. Two female siblings against me," Max bemoaned, but his buoyant tone belied his words.

Asha grinned as they arrived in the dining room, the fragrant smell of grilled chicken and the sight of the table full of food making her stomach growl.

Meeting Kade's pensive gaze, she smiled at him, trying to let him know silently that everything was okay.

He grinned back at her, his gorgeous blue eyes lighting up as he winked at her.

God, he was handsome. And she sat directly across from him at the table. She'd never had a better dinner with such a colorful and glorious view. He flirted with her outrageously, making her cheeks flush and causing the others to shoot her questioning looks. But the meal was boisterous and full of laughter, so unlike anything she'd ever experienced.

For Asha, it was her first real family dinner, and she tried to commit every detail to her memory for the future. She knew that moments like this, feeling this way, didn't last forever, right?

Her eyes met and held with Kade's, and he slowly nodded, as though he'd read her thoughts and was reassuring her that things could last for a lifetime. She sighed and lived for the moment, enjoyed the intimacy, and tried not to think about what the future might hold.

Because at the moment…everything was perfect.

Chapter 7

Several nights later, Kade lay in his enormous bed, sore, sleepless, and frustrated. Unfortunately, someone had leaked the news story that the long-lost sister of Max Hamilton and Maddie Hudson had been found. He and Asha had been hounded by reporters all day and he hadn't left the house. Instead, he had watched Asha create her designs on the wall of his home gym, his cock hard as granite, as he punished himself on the equipment. He'd tried like hell not to watch her, but he knew he'd been deluding himself, thinking he was only there to work out. Watching her had become a fascination he couldn't stop, didn't want to stop. Her whole body moved and swayed as she painted, every part of her involved in what she was creating. It was almost like watching her doing an exotic dance. The only thing hotter would have been if she'd taken her clothes off while she was doing it. But he had a vivid imagination, and damned if he couldn't conjure up the images of her doing just that as he ogled her while pretending he was there to just do his daily workout, a workout that had taken all damn day. No wonder his whole body ached. Yeah, he was used to brutal workouts, but they usually didn't last for eight damn hours.

Surprisingly, he was beginning to like the images she was creating on that wall. At first, he'd balked when she'd suggested painting a collection of his pictures from his football days in the gym. But Asha was passionate about her work, and she'd argued that he should celebrate his success as a football player and all he'd accomplished, remember all the things he'd done well when he was playing. She'd reminded him that football *had* been a big part of his life, and it was better to remember the pleasant things instead of dwelling on the negative. He'd relented, letting her have free rein to do whatever she wanted.

The images were copied from pictures of his glory days, and Asha brought them to life with her extraordinary talent. Rather than making him depressed about what he could no longer do, the paintings accented the camaraderie of the team, and the poignant moments he'd had with the guys from the Cougars. They were all happy, upbeat scenes that made him smile rather than making him feel depressed that he couldn't play football anymore. Most of the men who were with him on the wall were retired now, and Kade suspected that Asha knew that; she had probably researched every photo. The design was an upbeat tribute to some great football players who had moved on to do other things with their life.

Smiling in the dark, Kade wondered if her project in that particular room was Asha's way of telling him to celebrate, but move on. All of her designs meant something, and he was pretty sure she was trying to kick his ass into accepting reality and dealing with it via her artwork in the gym. Well, it was working, and he knew he needed to find a new purpose in his life. He just wished he knew exactly what it was.

Flipping onto his side, he punched his pillow, determined to get some sleep. He wouldn't think about Asha lying in her bed, right across the hall from him. He wondered if she was still wearing the new nightgown he'd gotten her when she was sick, or if she'd graduated to what Maddie and Mia had bought her. He had to admit, his sister and Maddie had much better taste when it came to clothes.

Even so, he loved seeing Asha in the clothing he'd bought her while she was sick, and he hadn't yet seen her wear anything other than the shirts and jeans he'd bought her in Nashville—except for the day when Maddie, Max, and Mia had come visiting and he'd handed her one of the shirts his sister had bought.

His stomach growled, reverberating noisily under the covers.

"Shit! I'm hungry," he said irritably, knowing he wasn't going to sleep anytime soon. He'd burned so much energy in the gym today that his body was clamoring for more food.

He tossed the sheets and blankets from his body and rose to his feet, striding to his bedroom door and yanking it open. He stopped for a moment, staring at Asha's door. Everything was dark, including her room. There was no light under her door, and he flipped on the hall light and made his way downstairs, stopping abruptly at the entrance to the kitchen.

Kade could see a sliver of light coming from the refrigerator, and it illuminated Asha's face as she stared at the contents within, a look of longing on her face.

What the hell is she doing?

Staying silent, the minutes ticked away as she seemed to be agonizing over something, but she didn't reach for anything. She just stayed immobile, her eyes roving over the inside of the fridge.

Unable to stay quiet any longer, Kade flipped on the light, causing Asha to let out a surprised *squeak* and slam the refrigerator closed. Holding a hand over her chest, she told him nervously, "You scared me."

"I'm sorry. I didn't mean to startle you. What the hell are you doing? And why didn't you turn the light on? You could have hurt yourself skulking around in the dark," he grumbled, unhappy with the thought of Asha tumbling down the stairs because she couldn't see where the hell she was going.

"I guess I didn't think about it," she answered, agitated. "I'm sorry. I'll go back to bed."

"Were you hungry? I'm starving. Do you want something?" he asked, walking to the fridge and opening the door. Mia had made sure the house was well-stocked with groceries before he came back from Nashville. Not only had she picked up the things he'd asked her to get for Asha, but she'd stocked up on groceries because he'd been gone for two months doing a favor for her husband.

"We already had dinner," Asha replied, shifting from one foot to the other nervously.

"Yeah. And it was delicious. But that was hours ago." Kade looked at Asha curiously. She had cooked tonight, making him some traditional Indian food, and he'd scarfed down the homemade dinner greedily. Asha was an excellent cook, but she hadn't eaten much. Come to think of it...she rarely did. "I made a pig of myself on your food. Did you get enough to eat?" he asked solemnly. "I thought there was food left over."

"You mentioned you were going to eat it for lunch tomorrow," she said uncomfortably.

Kade thought back to other meals. He'd grilled again the night before, and she'd eaten sparsely then, too. "I meant I'd eat it if it was still around. I'm not picky. I'll eat just about anything."

Asha stayed mute, staring up at him, her dark eyes confused. "I didn't want to eat your food."

"Fuck," Kade growled, enlightenment finally hitting his thick skull. He grabbed her by the shoulders lightly, letting the door of the fridge close behind him. "Asha...please tell me you aren't going hungry because you're afraid to eat." Kade felt suddenly nauseated, a lump forming in his stomach. Something was seriously wrong with this situation, and the thought that she might be going hungry made him crazy.

Breaking away from him, she started to move away as she murmured, "I eat."

Kade grasped her upper arm before she could move away, turning her back toward him. "Tell me what's wrong. You don't eat much, and you're too thin. Are you still feeling sick?"

She shook her head. "No. I'm not sick. I just don't want to eat more than my share," she retorted, her voice radiating with shame. "But I get hungry sometimes between meals."

Kade could almost feel the heat of his anger radiating from his body. "Your share is eating until you're stuffed, and then eating again whenever you're hungry. You eat like a goddamn bird. Why?"

"Because I don't want to eat food I haven't paid for," she replied, her voice suddenly defensive and angry.

Kade grasped her shoulders, shaking her lightly. "Have I ever made you feel like anything other than a guest who has the run of this house? Have I ever denied you anything you needed? Have I ever made you feel like you couldn't do any fucking thing you wanted here?" he asked her angrily, although the fury was directed at himself. He should have noticed that she wasn't eating enough. Problem was, he was used to being with Amy, and she ate mostly salad and lean meat to keep her model figure, but even she had splurged occasionally.

"No. Never. It isn't you, Kade," she answered tremulously, her head lowered so all Kade could see was the top of her head.

"Then for Christ's sake, tell me what it is, because the thought of you going hungry makes me want to punch myself for not noticing."

Asha raised her head slowly, finally looking him in the eye. "My foster parents used to feed me measured portions. They said they only received so much money to be my foster parents, and I could only have what I was allotted because food was expensive. The younger children, her children, ate dinner first and I served the family. I ate whatever was left, or my portion…whichever was less." She took a shaky breath in and continued, "I did the same when I was married, trying to save money on food. I guess it became a habit. I wasn't working for most of my marriage, so I didn't want to cause Ravi more expense, especially since I wasn't pregnant. I could get by with less food."

Kade slammed his fist down on the kitchen table hard enough to cause the table to bounce on its thin wooden legs, making Asha jump at the violent sound. "Fuck! Tell me you're joking!" he begged angrily, rage pulsating through his body. "You were a damn servant for your foster family, and you ate scraps of food? Then you did the same when you were married…and your husband never said anything?" It was unfathomable, and Kade's whole body shuddered with fury.

She shrugged. "I didn't want anything that I wasn't entitled to have," she said meekly.

Kade exploded. "You're entitled to eat, you were entitled to a fucking education because you have incredible talent, you're entitled to be treated like a beloved daughter and wife. That includes your idiot foster parents and your asshole of an ex-husband making sure you have everything you want and need."

Had everyone in her life done a number on her? Jesus Christ! The woman needed someone to teach her to feel worthy, and it was going to start with him.

Kade felt another stab of guilt as he thought about the look of longing on her face when he'd been watching her from the doorway. He'd neglected to see that in some of her habits, she was still conditioned to be a second-class citizen. Her foster parents had been evil, and her ex-husband was a selfish prick.

"Sit down," he demanded quietly, leading her to a chair and pulling it out for her.

She sat, asking anxiously, "Are you angry with me?"

Kade crouched beside her, wrapping an arm around her waist. "I'm angry at myself." He sighed heavily before continuing, "I want you to eat, Asha. I want you to eat whenever and whatever you want. There is no such thing as eating only what you think you deserve and going hungry in this house. My rule. I don't give a shit what anyone told you. It kills me that you ever went hungry in my home." He rose and started yanking stuff from the cupboards and fridge. "I don't cook a lot, but I make a great sandwich."

"Let me help you." Asha made to leap up from her chair.

"Sit down," he answered stubbornly, pushing on her shoulder until her ass hit the seat of the chair again. "I'm serving this time."

"It's your house. You shouldn't have to do this," Asha said uncomfortably.

"I want to." He wanted to pile food in front of her until she could barely see over the top of the mound. She'd eat, and then she'd eat some more. He never wanted to see that look of longing on her face again unless it was sexual. And he'd be more than willing to satiate *that* need, too.

He piled the sandwich high, loading it with every kind of fixings he could find. After placing it in front of her, he placed a napkin beside her plate. Rifling through the cupboard, he started piling various boxes of crackers and chips on the table.

What else?

"What were you looking at when I came in?" he asked anxiously, ready to pile the whole damn refrigerator on the table.

"A chocolate cake," she answered in a hushed and somewhat awed voice. "One with strawberries and slices of dark chocolate on top of the frosting."

Kade grinned. "The chocolate-strawberry torte. My favorite. Mia picked it up at our favorite bakery." He pulled it out and cut off two huge chunks and placed them on a plate, grabbed two forks and added the lot to the table. After pouring two tall glasses of milk, he finally sat, noticing that Asha was still staring at the food on the table. "Eat," he prompted. "If you don't devour that food yourself, I swear I'll wrestle you to the ground and force-feed you. You're never going hungry again. You're going to walk around stuffed every minute of the day," he told her earnestly.

Kade grinned as Asha put a hand to her mouth and stifled a giggle. "I can't eat all of this," she said, sounding amused.

Kade looked at the table piled high with food. "Eat as much as you can. That's part of your job from now on. No more skimping on food. I'll consider it an insult if you *don't* eat. There are obviously still things in your past that you need to recognize as wrong and get over them. We're resolving the food issue right fucking now."

She took a healthy sip of milk and started in on her monstrous sandwich. Kade opened a bag of chips and started feeding them to her between bites of her sandwich. Halfway through the sandwich he'd created, she pushed the plate away and put a hand to her flat belly. "I'm full."

Kade snatched the other half of the sandwich from the plate and pushed the cake in front of her. "Eat." Picking up the fork, he put it in her hand.

Her eyes lit up as she cut off a tiny piece. "I haven't eaten a lot of chocolate. This looks almost sinful."

Kade grinned at her, catching her eyes and holding them for a moment. "It is. But sinning can be so much more fun than being good all the time." He wolfed down the rest of the sandwich and started on his piece of cake.

He watched her while she ate, the rapt expression on her face almost erotic. She ate like she was climaxing every time she took a bite of the pastry, closing her eyes and savoring it before letting it slowly slide down her throat. His burgeoning cock twitched every time she let out a satisfied hum of pleasure.

I'm screwed. Every damn thing she does turns me on.

He yanked his eyes away from her, studying his own nearly empty plate. "Don't do something like this again, Asha. If you need or want something, all you have to do is say so. What happened to you wasn't right. You have to ask for what you want. I won't deny you anything. It makes me happy to please you," he said huskily.

"That confuses me," she admitted, pushing her empty plate away from her. "I'm not used to it."

"Get used to it," he said, shooting her a warning glance.

"I probably could. Very easily." She got up and started putting things away. "And I won't be with you forever. I'm not sure I really should get used to it. Life isn't easy out there, Kade. Not for a woman struggling to survive."

She'd never be struggling again. She'd never have to worry about where her next meal was coming from or where her next job would be. He'd make sure of it. "Your life isn't going to be like that again. You have family now. You have me."

He got up and put the dishes in the dishwasher, banging them a little harder than necessary, trying to get a grasp on his instinct to grab her up and make her his until she was completely convinced.

"I'm glad I have friends and family now. But I need to be able to know I can rely on myself," she answered stubbornly. "Putting my life into other people's hands hasn't been good for me."

"Maybe you just trusted the wrong damn people," he rumbled, slamming the dishwasher closed and turning to face her.

He heard her inhale sharply as she looked at him, her eyes scanning his body. "Oh, Kade. Your poor leg. It must have been so painful."

He looked down at himself, realizing he was dressed in nothing but a pair of black silk boxers. He hadn't bothered to put on clothes because he hadn't planned on seeing anyone else at one o'clock in the morning in his own house.

Her eyes were focused on his mangled leg, and he flinched. "I'm sorry. I would have covered it if I'd known you were down here."

Dammit! Asha was the last person he wanted to see his messed-up leg. Even healed, the scars were glaring and ugly. "Don't look at it," he snarled, moving closer to her and tipping her chin up. "I can't even stand to see it."

"It isn't the way it looks; it's the pain you must have suffered," she cried, her eyes filling with tears. "How did you bear it?" Dropping to her knees, Asha's fingertips stroked lightly over his scars.

"I didn't have much of a choice," he answered gruffly, his heart thundering from the touch of her fingers. Some of the feeling on his skin was gone from the scar tissue, but he could feel the fluttery, careful stroking on some of his leg.

She's not repulsed by my scars. All she cares about is the pain I felt.

Kade watched her carefully. Dressed in the silky nightgown he had bought her, she looked like an angel, her face revealing nothing but concern.

"And you worry about me being hungry when you've been through that much pain?" Asha scolded, standing again and facing him.

Kade wanted to tell her that it didn't hurt anymore, not nearly as much as the pain he was suffering from wanting her. "It's over."

He wanted to forget about that time in his life. His leg ached occasionally, but he'd survived.

"Does it still hurt? Tell me the truth."

Yeah. I hurt, but the pain isn't in my leg. I ache every fucking time I look at you.

"No," he replied huskily. "It's not that bad." *Not my leg, anyway.*

She moved closer to him and wrapped her arms around his waist. The feel of her hand on his bare skin nearly made him lose it. She was trying to comfort him for an old pain, but she was creating one just as acute. He wrapped his arms around her, feeling her softness against his hard body.

"I'm sorry, Kade. I wish this had never happened to you," she murmured against his chest.

"Shit happens," he replied casually, trying not to give in to the urge to carry her back to his bed and bury himself inside her warmth, take the comfort she was willing to give. But he didn't want her that way. He wanted it to be mutual, for her to burn for him as much as he did for her. She continued to cling to him, murmuring words into his chest that he didn't understand and suspected were Telugu, crooning them softly.

"You realize I don't understand a word you're saying," he told her, trying to contain the tender emotions that were bursting to get free.

"I know. I think it's better that way," she retorted, her voice amused. "And I really think you need to get over a few things from your own past. You're young, you're incredibly handsome, you can still walk, and you're alive. You survived. Other than the pain that I know you suffer sometimes, your leg doesn't matter. How it looks doesn't matter."

Kade knew Asha really meant what she said, and his soul began to heal a little bit more. He lowered his cheek to her hair, inhaling her floral scent and closing his eyes.

Kade wasn't certain exactly how long they stood that way, wrapped up together as though they were connected. He was pretty sure it was a fairly long period of time, but not long enough. His cock was hard, a reaction that was pretty much a certainty whenever Asha was close enough to feel, close enough to smell, but this wasn't a moment he wanted to think about his dick. Right now, he just wanted to wallow in Asha's sweetness, hold her close to his body and drink her in. Being near her had become an addiction, and satisfying her every want and need had become an obsession.

They finally parted and made their way back upstairs. He had to clench his fists to resist the urge to reach for her as she gave him a shy smile and closed the door of her bedroom. Kade flopped into his bed, which was suddenly much too lonely and big. It took him a very long time to finally fall into an exhausted sleep.

Chapter 8

The following week turned into some of the happiest days of Asha's life. She painted, not feeling rushed to complete the project, and she certainly wasn't worried about where her next meal was coming from. Kade was almost a pain in the ass about her eating. He was spending time in the Harrison offices now with Travis, but every moment he was home, he brought her food. Plying her with chocolate, decadent pastries, and calorie-laden desserts seemed to be one of his favorite activities. In between, he never seemed to run out of other food for her to try. If she wasn't careful, she'd soon be popping out of her jeans.

She'd started working out with him every morning, always in awe when he continued to pump weights after he was done with his cardio. Although she did a lot of walking, she was a wimp next to him, doing her time on the treadmill and the bike, completely exhausted when she was done. She finished, huffing and puffing, before Kade had even broken a sweat.

Stopping to stretch her back, Asha sighed as she stared at Kade's bedroom wall. After finishing the painting of a leopard in a rain forest on his den wall, she'd moved up to the master bedroom, still contemplating exactly what would fit *here*. There was nothing really intimate about his bedroom. It was a minimalist type of room, just like the rest of the house, and it lacked color.

She smiled as she remembered Kade telling her to paint every wall in the house, and his grimace as she'd told him that doing every wall was overkill. He could use some accent and color, maybe one wall in most rooms, but he didn't need *every* wall painted. Unhappy with her answer, he'd grumbled, but he hadn't mentioned it again.

He lets me be free to use my talent. He trusts me with his home.

Kade valued her opinion and he listened to her when she had an idea. He made her feel…important, and she carried that emotion close to her heart. No one had ever made her feel appreciated or valued, and Kade was slowly showing her that she had worth, that she *was* worthy of far more than she'd experienced in the past.

"Asha?" A deep baritone sounded near the door, startling her, and pulling her abruptly from her wandering thoughts.

Her eyes flew to him, and her breath caught as she saw Kade standing in the doorway with an amused grin.

Her hand to her chest, she said, "Sorry. I was thinking."

Looking incredibly handsome in the suit and tie he'd worn to the office, her heart lifted at the sight of him, still managing to be uniquely Kade by wearing a colorful maroon shirt and a tie with very ornate cornucopia for the upcoming Thanksgiving holiday. On Kade, it looked nothing less than masculine and splendid, an image that always made her heart smile. He had his own style, and he was completely comfortable with it. It was one of the sexiest things she'd ever seen.

"What were you thinking about?" he asked curiously, shedding the jacket of his suit and tossing it on the chair.

You. What else do I seem to always be thinking about these days?

"Your wall," she answered hastily, turning her eyes back to the wall she had been contemplating. She was way too preoccupied with Kade, and she needed to get him out of her brain. He was a client, and maybe a friend. But she couldn't think of him as anything more than that. "Did Travis like your new image?" she asked curiously, wondering what his twin had thought of Kade's bright shirt and tie.

Kade let out a bark of laughter as he undid the knot on the tie around his neck. "No. He said the tie and shirt weren't really a step up from my shirt with the dancing hotdogs that I wear to the office occasionally." He yanked the tie from around his neck and tossed it on top of his suit jacket. "How did I end up with a brother with no sense of style?" Kade asked mournfully. "Nothing but dark suits and ties. He looks like a funeral director. The only one who saves him from being completely morbid is his secretary, Ally, who he still insists on calling Alison even though she hates it. Or if she's really annoying him, she's Ms. Caldwell."

Asha laughed. "And what is she mostly?" She'd met Travis just the day before, and although he was cordial, he *was* rather intimidating. It was almost difficult to believe he and Kade were brothers, much less twins. The two of them were incredibly different.

"Ms. Caldwell. She's almost always in trouble with Travis," Kade answered wickedly. "But she challenges him. She's good for him. I think she's one of the few people in the office who isn't terrified of him."

"I'm surprised he hasn't fired her." Asha picked up Kade's tie and jacket, ready to put them in the dry-cleaning pile in the laundry room.

"I think he secretly likes her, in an antagonistic kind of way. And she's damn good at her job. Travis knows things at the office would descend into total chaos without her," Kade mused, sitting down on the bed to pull off his shoes. "Put those back or I'll put you over my knee," Kade growled. "You aren't my servant. I'll take care of them…eventually."

Asha's eyes shot to Kade's face. He was completely serious, and he wasn't happy. Flustered, she tried to think of how to explain that sometimes she *liked* to do things for him. "I was just—"

"I'll give you three seconds to put them back," he said with deadly calm.

"Kade, I don't mind—"

"One." His voice was serene, but laced with warning.

Oh, how Asha wanted to argue. She didn't fear Kade, and she wanted to help him once in a while. He'd done so much for her. She didn't feel like she *had* to clean up after him. It was so different when she actually was doing something for someone who appreciated her. She wanted to help him, and she liked touching and smelling anything that belonged to him. His scent was so intoxicating, so masculine.

"Two." The warning note in his voice was more pronounced. He dropped the other shoe and his eyes roved over her bare legs, exposed in a pair of old jeans that she had cut off to wear to work around the house. His eyes slowly moved upward, his gaze caressing her breasts and the nipples that were beginning to pebble with excitement beneath her old red tank top.

"What if I want to do it? What if I do it just because I love to handle your clothes because they smell like you?" she answered in a breathless rush, knowing they were in a struggle that was about so much more than just her waiting on him. She was actually calling his bluff, daring him to touch her. He'd been remote, careful...and she wanted to see his eyes torrid with passion again, the way they had been when he'd taken her to paradise in the kitchen with his mouth and fingers. The hand holding his jacket and tie were trembling, but she didn't move. Heat pooled between her thighs, and her nipples were as hard as diamonds. She stood there, waiting.

"Three," he growled, springing off the bed and wrapping a corded, muscular arm around her waist. Plucking the jacket and tie out of her hands, he tossed them on the floor and pulled her down on the bed, where she lay sprawled on top of his brawny, ripped body.

Asha struggled to breathe, the feel of his hot, taut, hard muscle beneath her making her heart stutter and rendering her completely breathless. Pushing back the curtain of hair that had tumbled down from its confining clip and into her face, she looked at him, shocked. His arm was still clamped around her waist, holding her prisoner on top of him. And his eyes were like pools of deep blue fire.

"I'm sorry. You don't understand," she said tremulously.

Kade removed the clip that was now hanging from her hair carefully and tossed it to the floor. "You can't say shit like that and not expect me to respond," Kade said huskily, spearing his fingers into her hair. "If you like the way I smell, handle the real thing," he demanded. "Touch me, Asha, before I lose my mind. Fuck the clothes; I need your hands on *me* more."

It was a command she didn't want to and couldn't resist. Her trembling fingers started working the buttons on his shirt, desperate to find his warm, bare skin. She fumbled, unable to look away from his intent expression. Having him need her, if only for a little while, was intoxicating and potent. No man had ever looked at her the way Kade was, and her body was answering his beckoning pheromones, the need to have him inside her almost painful.

"I'm not sure how you want to be touched," she said nervously, her fingers itching to feel his hot skin.

Kade groaned as she pulled his shirt open and tentatively placed her palms on his muscled chest. "It doesn't matter. Any way you want."

Asha moved to straddle his body and wriggled down further, her smoldering core cradling his engorged cock. His skin was fiery and smooth beneath her fingertips, and she feathered her hands over his chest, hesitantly at first, sighing at the feel of all his leashed strength and power beneath her.

Suddenly, it didn't matter that she shouldn't be doing this or that she was only here for a job. It might be a mistake to get too attached to Kade, but the fiery need that seethed between them couldn't be denied any longer. Just once, Asha wanted to feel what it would be like to be needed, desired in the way she knew Kade wanted her.

"These are beautiful." Her fingers stroked over the tattoo of a colorful phoenix rising from fire on the right side of his chest. After she finished tracing the fierce phoenix, she moved to the other side of his chest to stroke over the rendering of a dragon, predominantly black, but with red, orange, and dark blue intermingled in the scales. There was a fiery football gripped in his ragged teeth. "I suppose this one was a reminder to win your games?"

"The guys all called me 'The Dragon' because I always wore my lucky dragon shirt on game days," he replied raggedly. "Some bastard stole it from the locker room, so I got a permanent tat because I didn't have my shirt anymore."

Asha moved her fingers back over the phoenix. It reminded of her of her butterfly, only his creature was soaring with its wings fully spread, straight out of the fire licking at its long, feathered tail. "And this one?"

"Travis has it, too. We were together and drinking one night and decided to get it during the scandal of the death of our parents. It's the only time I've actually seen Travis drunk. We swore we'd rise above being the crazy Harrison family."

"You did," Asha answered quietly, admiring Kade's ferocity to overcome his past. It made her all the more determined to become independent and strong. Mia, Kade, and Travis might still have some remnants that haunted them from their childhood, but they'd all risen like the fiery phoenix on Kade's chest.

Kade groaned as Asha started to move lower, tracing the happy trail of light hair that ran from his navel to the top of his pants. His body was sculpted so beautifully, and the tattoos just added to his masculine aura.

Fire licked at her entire body, demanding that she have this man, and she was tired of denying herself.

Her mind made up, she rolled to his side and pulled the tank top over her head. She was braless and it only took her a moment to wriggle out of her shorts and panties, dropping them to the floor. Finally, she turned to look at Kade, meeting his eyes with a courage she didn't know she had. "I want you inside me. Will you do it?"

Kade gaped at her, his gaze skimming over her nude body before his eyes collided with hers. "You just got naked, and *now* you're asking me that question?"

"Well...will you?" she asked, a little more uncomfortable now with her assumption that he would.

"Sweetheart, being inside you is the subject of most of my fantasies," Kade answered hoarsely, rising to his feet by the side of the bed, his hungry eyes never leaving hers.

"Only most of them?" she asked nervously as he yanked off his shirt and let it fall on top of the growing pile of discarded clothing.

He shot her a wicked grin as he shed his pants. "It's one of the highlights, but it's not the only thing I've dreamed about doing."

"What else is there?" Asha asked, confused, laying down on her back and parting her legs. "I'm ready," she told him anxiously, her breath catching as Kade kicked off his boxers and stood next to the bed completely nude. "Oh, God. You're hotter than I ever imagined," she blurted out as her gaze caressed every sculpted muscle, every perfect curve of his body. Her pussy flooded with heat as she saw his enormous cock bouncing off rock-hard abs. "And you're…big."

He put one knee on the bed. "What are you doing?" he asked huskily.

"I said I was ready," she answered, her body pulsating with need as she looked at him. "I'm ready for you to be inside me."

"No you aren't," he answered in a slow drawl. "But you will be."

"I'm ready," she insisted, wondering what he was waiting for, and wishing he'd get on with it. She was beyond ready to be joined to him, and she'd never felt this need for any man before.

Kade let out a strangled sound, a cross between a groan and laugh, and pulled her up on her knees, one powerful arm around her waist. "You're so innocent," he growled, spearing his hands in her hair and pulling her upper body flush with his. "Baby, you don't need to just assume the position and have it over with in moments."

Asha trembled as his powerful body made complete contact with her smaller form, engulfing her in heat. "I'm not that innocent. I was married for seven years," she huffed.

"Yeah. And I need you to forget whatever it is you did when you were married and just feel. Can you do that?" His hot mouth trailed down the sensitive skin at the side of her neck, making her shiver.

"Yes," she whispered longingly. Obviously, there was so much more to learn about being with a man than she had discovered in her marriage. "Tell me what you want, Kade." She wasn't sure how to please him, but she wanted to so very much.

"I just want you," Kade answered hotly, his hand stroking down her back and cupping her ass. He brought her needy core against his cock with a groan.

Asha couldn't wait any longer. She threaded her fingers through his hair and greedily pulled his mouth to hers, letting instinct and the strange connection she felt with him take over completely. Kade responded immediately, his lips fusing with hers, his hands moving to hold her head in place while he ravaged her mouth, taking charge immediately. He didn't stop with one kiss. The first impassioned embrace lead to another, and then another, neither one being able to get enough of the other. The banked flames between them had finally been fanned, and they were caught in a raging inferno that neither one of them could subdue.

She ended up sprawled on her back again. Their limbs tangled as their mouths stayed fused together. Kade cupped her breasts, teasing the hard, sensitive nipples, sending a jolt of electricity straight to her pussy.

Pulling his lips from hers, he rasped, "Tell me that you want this as much as I do, Asha."

"I do," she moaned, her body writhing beneath his, her hips rising in a silent plea. "I need you."

His mouth came down on one of her nipples, his teeth nipping, his tongue stroking. Asha panted, her body completely unused to this kind or this level of arousal. "I didn't know it could feel like this," she whispered to herself.

Kade heard her. Lifting his head, he laved his tongue in the valley between her breasts before he said harshly, "We're just starting, so you'll be feeling a whole lot more before long." His fingers pinched her nipples lightly, his tongue following the sting of pain. "Your breasts are perfect."

"Small," Asha answered in a breathless voice.

"Just right," Kade argued, cupping them in his hands. "Your nipples remind me of rich, milk chocolate. Did I ever tell you how addicted I am to chocolate?"

It was a question that wasn't meant to be answered, and Asha wasn't able to speak as Kade drew each nipple into his mouth, one after the other, sucking and stroking with his mouth and tongue. He seemed to know just how to touch them, how to make her absolutely crazy. No one had ever worshipped her breasts, and that was exactly what Kade was doing, making her lose every insecurity she'd ever had about her not being particularly abundant. Obviously, he found them alluring, and that was all that mattered to her at the moment.

She whimpered as Kade moved lower, his mouth and tongue tasting the skin of her belly. His hands caressed her legs before gripping them securely and opening her to him. Asha felt the air hit the sensitive flesh between her thighs as Kade moved, going lower, one of his large hands sliding up her thigh and using his fingers to penetrate the already saturated folds of her pussy.

Asha knew she should have been mortified. Kade's head was directly between her thighs, his fingers delving into her pussy, but she felt nothing but a clenching in her gut, a need so volatile that she raised her hips, begging for something more. "Please, Kade." Her voice was desperate, tortured. She'd never felt this way before, never had a man pleasure her in this way, and it was akin to both torture and ecstasy. How was it that she was twenty-seven years old and had never felt this kind of arousal? Asha felt as if this was her sexual awakening. What had once been a duty was now a pleasure beyond her comprehension.

This is what I missed. This is what I always yearned for, but never knew exactly what was missing.

"Please what?" Kade asked in a low, aroused voice. "Voice it out loud. Tell me what you need."

"Touch me harder. Touch me there," Asha told him desperately, surprised that she could actually ask for what she wanted. But with Kade, she knew she could. It wasn't dark, there was no shame, and he was making her feel wanted, needed and so very feminine.

His fingers moved, one tip flicking across her clit. "Like that?" he asked in a muffled voice, his tongue stroking the crease between her thigh and her pussy.

"Yes. But harder," she begged, not recognizing her own needy voice.

"I'm going down on you, Asha. I have to taste your orgasm when you come," Kade said harshly, right before his tongue and mouth started to devour her.

Asha's ass came completely off the bed, and Kade slipped his hands beneath it, cupping it to draw her harder against his mouth, groaning into her pussy as he used his lips and mouth to make her completely lose control. "Kade. I can't—" She wanted to tell him she couldn't breathe, but it wasn't true. She was panting, a moan escaping as she stopped fighting the ecstasy of what he was doing to her and let herself just…feel, exactly the way he had asked her to do. Her hands gripped his head, desperate for release. "Please," she pleaded.

His tongue moved over her clit a little harder, a little faster, making her even more frenzied. She came apart just when she was certain she was going to lose her mind, her body rocking with the force of her climax.

"Kade." She gasped his name as she fisted his hair, letting Kade own her body during those moments, his tongue still moving over her clit, his mouth savoring every drop of her explosive orgasm.

She was still quivering when Kade crawled up her body. Both of them were slick with sweat, but she suspected most of it was hers. Dear God…she'd never felt anything like what Kade had just done to her. Her heart was still racing, pounding in her throat, making her unable to speak. Kade's eyes were turbulent and fierce as he looked down at her with male satisfaction. "You're beautiful," he said in a husky, awed voice.

"Nobody has ever told me that before," she admitted in a shaky voice. "No one has ever made me feel the way you do. You actually make me believe that."

"Well, believe it. You're fucking perfect. And your body responds to mine like it was made for me," he said possessively, threading her hair through his fingers. "And just for the record...I've never felt like this either," he added emphatically, his eyes devouring her, making her even more hungry for his possession.

Asha wanted him inside her at that very moment more than she wanted her next breath. Opening her mouth to speak, all she could manage to say was, "Fuck me, Kade. Please." Those words had never left her mouth before, but it was so easy to say to Kade when she saw the desire burning in his eyes. He wanted her to want him as much as he wanted her, and she wanted him to know that she already did.

"If I fuck you, you're mine. I don't know if I can ever let you go," he rasped. "I'm not sure I can anyway."

Asha's heart was thundering as she stroked her hands down his arms, feeling the leashed power and tension in his body. "I have so far to go, Kade. There's so much I have to do to find myself." She wanted to tell him right then and there that she was his forever, that she'd never feel this way about any other man. Although she knew how she felt about him, he didn't deserve a woman who was broken. "I'm still damaged."

"So am I," he answered honestly, his look determined. "But I don't give a fuck. We'll heal each other. I'll give you everything you need to be whole again. You belong with me."

Asha ached to believe him, her yearning for him soul deep. Stifling all the words she wanted to say, she answered, "Then take me. Please."

"I don't have condoms. I haven't been with a woman in years and I'm clean. And I don't plan to be with any other woman again," he said, his words a declaration.

"I'm barren. I'm safe. And I trust you," she panted, her body begging for his possession.

"You're not barren. I hate that expression, and it doesn't apply to you," Kade rasped, his cock rubbing against her folds as he thrust his hips forward. "You might be unable to have a child, but your body is my idea of paradise."

Asha gasped in shock and pleasure as Kade grasped her hips and entered her in one smooth stroke. He was built big, and he filled her to capacity, stretching internal muscles she hadn't realized she had.

"Fuck! You feel so damned incredible." He groaned, a sound of pure ecstasy. "Wrap your legs around my waist. Take everything you want from me. Whatever you need. Take your pleasure from me."

Asha complied, wanting to tell him that she already had everything she wanted. With Kade buried deep inside her, joined to her, she didn't think she could burn any hotter. Every nerve in her body was alive and electric as his cock entered and retreated, claiming her as no man ever had.

I love you. I love you.

She couldn't say the words out loud, but they were pounding through her head, matching the pummeling thrusts of his cock, making her frantic to climax. Every emotion was on overload, and she wrapped her legs tighter around him, her arms cinched around his broad shoulders. Whimpering with need, her short fingernails dug into his back, the pleasure so acute that she couldn't bear it. "Please. I need—"

"You need me to make you come," Kade told her, his voice harsh with need. "Only me. Tell me that's what you want."

"Yes. Yes. I need you. Just you," she answered emphatically. "Now do it," she demanded. "I can't take anymore."

"You can take it. You can take me." Kade rolled, his cock deep inside her, until she was sprawled on top of him. He took her hands and helped her sit up, keeping their fingers entwined. "Ride me," he said, his jaw tight, teeth clenched. It was a command, not a request.

Asha squirmed on top of him. "How?" This was new, something she'd never done before, and it was both frightening and powerful at the same time.

"Fuck me. Take me inside of you and ride my cock," he growled. "Hard and deep."

The look on his face was anguished, aroused, and complete-ly intoxicating. Asha's female instincts kicked in, watching his expression as she moved sensuously on his cock. The angle was different and he went deep as she sunk down onto him, rolling her hips as she plunged. She moaned as the walls of her channel stretched and contracted, as though they were hungry to swallow him deep inside her. The pleasure of having Kade this immersed inside her was earth-shattering and incredible, and Asha could feel the erotic pleasure course through her as she kept pulling back and taking him back inside her, over and over again. She squeezed Kade's fingers tightly, her body strung as tightly as a bow. "Oh God, I can't stand it," Asha cried, her body so tense, every nerve pulsating, until she wanted to scream with pleasure as she increased the speed of her thrusts.

Kade let go of her hands and reached for her breasts, pinching them lightly, making her feel the vibrating pleasure clear to her toes. Taking her hands again, he placed her hands over her nipples. "Touch them. Whatever feels good," he demanded.

Too close to climax to even think of feeling embarrassed, Asha took over working her breasts, pinching her nipples lightly, moaning her pleasure as Kade grasped her hips and took control. Holding her steady, he thrust up into her with powerful surges, groaning beneath her as he filled her over and over. "Jesus, you're so hot and tight that I never want to come." Kade panted harshly, the look on his face one of pure male erotic ecstasy.

Kade changed his position slightly, stimulating her clit with every stroke of his cock. His eyes were smoldering blue as he watched her touching herself as she whimpered and moaned her pleasure. "Christ! I can't last much longer." His plunges became deeper, harder, the stimulation to her clit more forceful. He moved one hand from her hip and pushed it close to the spot where they were joined, his thumb joining the friction of his cock, the stimulation to her clit so exquisite that Asha cried out. "Kade!"

Asha imploded, screaming Kade's name and digging her short nails deeply into his shoulders as she rode the waves of her climax, the pulsations going on for what seemed like forever. She milked Kade's cock with her contractions, and he let out a rapturous groan and pulled her mouth down roughly to his in a kiss that left her breathless, spilling his warm release deep inside her.

Their bodies still connected, Asha sprawled on top of his heaving chest, her body a completely mindless heap of quivering flesh.

"I've never—that was—" Asha stammered, trying to put into words the way she was feeling...and failing. "I didn't know it could be like that," she ended up saying breathlessly.

"It's never happened like that for me either, baby," Kade answered, his voice husky and raw.

Kade stroked her back, both of them trying to recover their breath. Words were inadequate, and Asha gave up trying to verbalize her tangled emotions. She just lay there quietly with Kade, savoring the afterglow of an experience so incredible that it had shattered her world. After she could breathe again, she said teasingly, "I've watched you do a lot more cardio and never break a sweat."

"It's you," Kade answered mischievously. "Your incredible body nearly gives me a heart attack. You'll play hell with my ego. I pride myself on stamina, but what just happened goes beyond physical strength."

Asha actually giggled; the thought of any man lusting after her body so intensely was almost inconceivable to her. But Kade obviously did. The same way she lusted after him. What had just happened, they had experienced together. She was sure of it. "I guess you'll have to work at improving," she told him, still slightly breathless.

Kade brought his hand down on her backside with a playful *whack*. "You're getting awfully cheeky and bossy. Now you're really bruising my ego. Do I need improvement?"

She lifted her head and looked at him. "No. What just happened was the most incredible thing I've ever felt in my life. It was perfect," she told him honestly.

All trace of humor gone, he answered, "Ditto, sweetheart." He pushed the hair back from her face and kissed her sweetly, slowly, like he had all the time in the world and it was the most important thing he had to do.

Asha kissed him back, knowing her life had just changed irrevocably, and she'd never be the same.

Later that night, she redid her henna tattoo, and her butterfly emerged just a little more.

Chapter 9

"I want you to help me locate Asha's ex-husband and her foster parents," Kade said with a deadly calm, looking from one man to the others sitting in his living room on Thanksgiving Day. He was hosting at his home. The women had kicked them all out of the kitchen today and given them clean-up duty, and Max, Sam, Simon, and Travis all looked at him, perplexed.

"Why?" Max asked curiously, taking a slug of the beer in his hand and giving Kade a confused look. "I thought she didn't have anything to do with any of them anymore."

Kade shuddered, the emotions he was trying to hold in check beating at him to let them come to the surface. Briefly, he tried to explain some of the abuse Asha had suffered, the men sitting around him listening intently. Kade took a long swallow of his beer before he finished, "I've seen the scars on her body, and I remember the doctor mentioned that he saw what looked like old rib fractures on her chest x-ray when she had pneumonia. I didn't think anything of it at the time, thinking maybe she'd had an accident and they'd healed. But now, I'm thinking they weren't caused by a damn accident." Just thinking about Asha's ex-husband beating her hard enough to break her ribs and leaving some of the scars he'd seen on her gorgeous body made him clench his fist around the bottle of beer in his hand. For a minute, he wondered if it might shatter.

"I'll help you," Max answered dangerously. "And I'm not even going to ask how you saw scars on her body."

"Kill the bastard," Simon grunted.

"I'm in," Sam said, his voice low and threatening.

"Not happening," Travis contradicted casually.

Four sets of angry male eyes shifted in his direction.

"What the fuck? I'd have thought you'd be the last one to have any qualms about this!" Kade slammed his empty beer on the coffee table, not giving a damn if it left a mark.

Travis shrugged, looking relaxed and in complete control of himself sitting in Kade's recliner. "I don't. He deserves to die for what he did to Asha. But you aren't doing this for Asha; you're doing it for yourself. Granted, I don't know her well, but she doesn't appear to be the type of woman who wants her brother, brother-in-law, and his friends to go to jail for murder." Travis heaved a beleaguered, masculine sigh. "He can be destroyed in other ways, pay for what he's done to her."

Kill. Kill. Kill. Kade wasn't sure much would placate his protective madness except death to the man who had beaten Asha nearly to death…more than once. Burying his head in his hands, he groaned, "I don't think I can be satisfied with anything else. Just the fact that he beat her hard enough to probably leave her close to death makes me insane."

"Me either," Max rasped.

"He needs to be wiped off the earth," Simon commented gruffly.

"Agreed," Sam echoed adamantly.

"For Christ's sake…I'm surrounded by some of the most brilliant, richest men in America, and you're all acting like idiots. Put your emotions aside and think with your heads," Travis said harshly. "You all have too damn much to lose to do anything else. You have kids or children on the way, women you care about."

"I can't just leave it," Kade replied, his voice hostile. "Yeah, I'm thinking of Asha, but he might kill the next woman he gets involved with."

A rumble of agreement echoed through the room.

"I'm not suggesting that you leave it. I'm suggesting that you put your emotions aside and use your head," Travis drawled. "The last thing Asha needs is more chaos and guilt in her life."

A pang of remorse stabbed at Kade's conscience. He knew Travis was right, but he couldn't seem to control his need to seek some kind of justice for Asha, one that involved severe pain and suffering to her ex-husband.

It had only been a few days since Asha had given him her body for the first time and rocked his world, but they'd made up for lost time by touching each other every chance they had. He couldn't seem to *not* touch her when she was anywhere near him. In fact, the urge to get up and go to the kitchen just to see her, make sure she was okay, was almost irresistible.

"I suppose you have a plan," Max said slowly, glaring at Travis.

Travis shot a superior look back at Max. "I generally do," he answered arrogantly. "I happen to use the head *above* my waist when it comes to women, unlike the rest of you."

"Not always," Kade reminded him hotly. "Not when it comes to Mia." Other than Travis, only Max would understand his statement because he was the only other one who knew that Travis was more than willing to kill when it came to Mia's safety.

"Unfortunate accident," Travis answered nonchalantly. "And Mia's safety was threatened."

Simon and Sam looked on, confused, but didn't comment.

Unfortunate accident, my ass. Kade had no doubt Travis had known exactly what he was doing when the man stalking Mia just happened to have his "unfortunate accident" that left him conveniently dead, never to bother their sister ever again. "I'm listening. But no guarantee that I still won't kill the bastard," Kade said sharply, his guts still telling him he needed to hurt the one who had hurt Asha.

Max folded his arms and pierced Travis with a stubborn look. "Let's hear it."

Sam and Simon grumbled, but agreed to hear Travis out.

With a satisfied smile, Travis began to talk.

Asha replaced the security phone by the door on its cradle and hugged baby Ginny a little tighter. Ginny Helen Hudson was sleeping peacefully in her arms. She loved the smell and feel of the infant, the trust the tiny being had given her by falling asleep while Asha had rocked her. Named after both of her grandmothers, Asha thought she was the most adorable infant she'd ever seen.

"Why would someone want to talk to me?" she muttered to the sleeping infant as though the baby would answer her. "I don't even know anyone here."

Turning away from the door, she walked back into the living room where the women were taking up residence while the guys were on cleaning duty after they had all indulged greedily of the Thanksgiving dinner. Fighting down the instinct to go to the kitchen and help because she was still uncomfortable with the idea of men in the kitchen, she reluctantly handed baby Ginny back to Kara with a frown. "Some lady wants to talk to me. A doctor. Kade's security agent said he checked her ID and she was legitimate. Apparently she knew my father and wants to give me something that belonged to him."

"What are you going to do?" Mia asked, her voice concerned.

Asha shrugged nervously. "I told him to let her come up to the house. She's alone. I can't let her leave if she's claiming to know my real father. I know so little about him. If she does know him, she can fill in some information, tell me more about him and maybe my mother."

"She could be a reporter in disguise," Maddie retorted, her voice sounding disgusted.

"Or just curious. There was enough coverage in the gossip rags about your discovery," Kara murmured as she repositioned the sleeping baby Ginny back in her lap.

The doorbell rang, and Asha flinched nervously. Had the woman really known her real father? And if she had known her father, she probably knew her mother, too. Why, after all these years, would she come here?

"I'll get it," Mia said hastily and jumped up from her seat on the couch to jog for the door.

Asha knew she could have answered the door herself, but confusion kept her feet planted on the carpet, the other three women looking at her anxiously.

Mia returned moments later, followed by an older Indian woman. The woman was dressed with casual elegance in a trendy pantsuit of muted fall colors, her hair gathered in a loose knot on the top of her head. Her age was hard to judge, but Asha could see some gray hairs peeking out of coal black tresses.

She stopped in front of Asha, her smile warm and comforting. "*Namaste*," Asha welcomed her softly in Hindi, India's national language. She wasn't certain exactly what to say to the woman, and not sure whether or not she even spoke Telugu.

Smiling wider, the woman echoed, "*Namaste*." She paused briefly before continuing in English. "You look very much like Navin and are as beautiful as Alice." She gently cupped Asha's cheek before dropping her hand and adding, "I knew you'd grow up beautiful even when you were a baby. You stole everyone's heart."

"Did we meet?" Asha asked curiously.

"Yes. But you wouldn't remember me. You were still an infant." The woman's English was lightly accented, but perfect.

"So you really did know my father," Asha said softly, offering the older woman a seat and sitting in a chair across from her.

"Yes. May I speak in front of your friends?" The woman looked around at Maddie, Kara, and Mia.

Asha nodded and introduced her sister, sister-in-law, and Kara, explaining that Mia's husband, Max, and Maddie were also Alice's children.

"It's wonderful to meet you all. I'm Devi Robinson." Looking at Maddie, she added, "I've heard of you, Dr. Hudson, and the wonderful work you do with your clinic."

Maddie nodded her thanks and replied, "I've heard of you, too. You're a psychiatrist. A very good one. I've read a lot of your case studies and articles."

"I am a doctor of psychiatry, a dream that never would have happened had it not been for Asha's father," she acknowledged in a fond voice. "How much do you know of your father's work to help Indian female students, Asha?"

Flabbergasted, Asha gaped at her. "He was an engineer," she answered, baffled by the woman's words.

Devi nodded. "He was. But he was also an activist for the rights of Indian women. And your mother supported him in the cause. They never formed an official organization, but he helped a lot of female students here in the United States, including myself. Navin Paritala was one of the best men I've ever known. He gave very selflessly to Indian women here in various bad circumstances. His only request was that we all someday give the money back to his daughter for her education when the time came." The woman rummaged in her purse, pulling an envelope from the contents. "None of us could ever locate you. You were whisked off to a foster family very quickly after your parents died, and we weren't allowed to know where you were. All of us have looked for years, but we couldn't locate you. When I saw the article about you being a half-sibling to Dr. Hudson and Mr. Hamilton, I had to find you. We owe you this." Devi handed Asha the envelope with a smile. "There were ten of us, and we all kept in contact. It's turned into a substantial sum."

Asha looked at the envelope and opened it with trembling fingers. The check from the bank was over two hundred thousand dollars. Her head began to spin and her heart pounded. "This isn't mine," she denied, trying to hand the check back to Devi.

The woman pushed Asha's hand away, refusing to take back the check. "It belonged to your father and mother. He helped all of us financially when we were in trouble. The money now belongs to you. Honestly, all of us are relieved we can finally pay back the debt. Your father gave us our freedom. That was much more valuable than money. When we all finished school, we all put the money in a joint account for you. It's been there for many years. None of us needs the money, Asha. And it belongs to you."

"What did Asha's father and my mother do to help you, Dr. Robinson—if you don't mind me asking?" Maddie asked quietly.

"I don't mind at all," Devi said, smiling broadly. "I fell in love with an American man, and my parents found out. They threatened to pull me out of school here and bring me back to India to marry someone from our caste, a man older than me and known to be cruel. Navin and Alice paid my school fees and helped me stay here. Dennis and I married and have two wonderful children, a daughter and a son, a mix of American and Indian just like Asha. Dennis is an architect."

"Is that hard for your children, being mixed?" Asha asked tremulously, curious about others like her.

"No," Devi answered fondly. "I teach them the good things about my country, but they're ultimately very progressive Americans. Both of them plan on going to medical school," she finished proudly. "Tell me how you were brought up after we lost track of you, Asha. Did you go to college? What do you do?"

Tears filled Asha's eyes as she looked at Devi, now knowing that her father wouldn't be very proud of her. She tried to speak, but failed.

Maddie, Mia, and Kara told Devi about Asha's upbringing and her arranged marriage.

"Oh, Asha!" Devi exclaimed, her eyes filling with tears. "I'm so sorry. That's not at all what your mother and father would have wanted. It seems so unfair that you ended up being treated that way after your own father gave us our freedom." Devi's voice was distressed, and she went to her knees beside Asha and gathered her into a hug. "Thank God you're still very young and you broke your ties. You can find your own way with the money we were able to pay back."

Asha cautiously hugged the woman back, asking quietly, "What do you think my father would have wanted for me?"

Devi slowly released Asha and returned to her seat as she said adamantly, "He would have wanted you to pursue the dream of your heart, whatever it may be. He wanted your happiness." She looked at Maddie, adding, "He knew your mother had two other children from her first marriage that she had to give up. Navin and Alice looked for both you and Mr. Hamilton, but were never able to discover where you were. I don't think they wanted to rip you away from adoptive parents, but they wanted to know you were okay. They were never able to find your records or get any information about you."

"We survived. And we all finally found each other," Maddie replied with a smile, sounding like that was all she wanted to tell the older woman. "So our mother did finally find a happy life with Asha's father?"

Devi nodded. "For the time they had together...yes. Navin and Alice loved each other very much. I think loving Navin changed your mother quite profoundly. I remember Alice telling me that she didn't like the woman she had been before, and Navin was her third marriage. I don't think she ever wanted to give you and Max up, but she thought you'd have a better life without her. She said she couldn't even afford to feed you and Max. I hope you can forgive her, Dr. Hudson. In the end, she was a good woman who helped her husband fight for women in bad circumstances. The love of a good man can change a woman, and I think in your mother's case that's exactly what happened."

"I'm not sure she was ever really bad," Maddie said sadly. "Just downtrodden. She and my father were poor, and I think she did what she needed to survive when my father died. I don't know much about her second marriage, but I'm assuming it wasn't good either. I'm glad she got lucky the third time, and I'm glad I got a sister out of the deal," Maddie said with a soft smile at Asha.

"My father and mother wouldn't be proud of me," Asha whispered to herself. Discovering that her father had been so progressive, so adamant about women being treated equally, made her stomach sink in dismay at the realization that she had failed him. What would he have thought of her past, of the abuse she had put up with from Ravi, of the treatment she'd endured as what she thought she deserved from both her foster parents and her ex-husband? He'd have been so disappointed in her.

"He would have been very proud," Devi replied sternly, having heard Asha's low comment. "You survived, even in very bad circumstances. I know Navin would be sad that he hadn't been there for you, but he would have been proud that you broke away and survived."

"I'm not sure who I am," Asha answered earnestly, looking Devi directly in the eyes. "I was raised very conventional Indian, yet I was born in America to an American mother and a progressive Indian father. I'm American, yet I don't feel like I am."

"You'll find your way. I'll help you," Devi said softly, extracting a business card from her purse and handing it to Asha. "If you can't speak to me about it, you can talk to my colleague. She's younger, but is an American with Indian blood just like you. It might be easier for you to talk to someone who never knew your father." Devi stood. "I'm sorry I interrupted your Thanksgiving, but I couldn't wait any longer to see you and repay you. I have to get back home. My husband is cooking our Thanksgiving dinner."

"Another man in the kitchen," Asha muttered.

Devi laughed softly. "Yes. And my son is helping him."

Asha shook her head. "How did you get used to it? You were raised in India."

"A little at a time," Devi answered, amused. "It's very easy to get used to once you've had the chance to be an equal partner, but it takes time to actually feel like one. Give yourself time, Asha."

Asha stood, realizing that at some point all of the men had joined them. After they all quickly introduced themselves, Max and Maddie walked Devi to the door, asking a few final questions about their mother. Asha started to follow, but was pulled up short by Kade, his arm tight around her waist.

"You okay?" he asked gruffly.

Was she okay? It was going to take awhile for her to process everything she'd just learned. She held up the check she had received from Devi. "I have money," she answered flatly, not quite able to believe the funds actually belonged to her.

"I heard. We all tried to give you privacy, but we heard the doorbell from the kitchen and eavesdropped pretty shamelessly," Kade said bluntly.

"My parents loved me, Kade. They cared," she answered tearfully. God, that was the most astonishing thing of the whole afternoon. "My father was a progressive. He actually helped Indian women in trouble. He was a good man."

"I know, sweetheart. Didn't you already know he was a good man?" Kade said huskily, pulling Asha against his chest and cuddling her close.

If she was honest with herself, Asha had assumed that she was probably of little importance to him because she was a girl child, and that her father was like the other Indian men in her life.

Her dad had made it his mission to see women treated well—equally, even—and he had liberal values. He...an Indian man...had helped women in trouble so they could follow their dreams. She shook her head against Kade's chest. "Not like that. I never imagined he was that good."

As Kara, Simon, Sam, Travis, and Mia looked on, Asha rested her head against Kade's chest and wept.

Chapter 10

Asha folded the last shirt she had bought for herself and placed it on the top of her new suitcase with a sigh. She hadn't packed the clothes that Maddie and Mia had bought, thinking she'd work it out with them later. They were too extravagant, and she was pretty much a casual woman. Her jeans, sandals, and shirts were pretty much her norm. She was a painter, and the outfits weren't something she'd normally wear. If she could get Maddie to take them back, her sister could get a refund. She hadn't worn any of them except the red shirt.

Kade's walls were complete, and she couldn't kid herself anymore about leaving. There wasn't one more wall that she could do in his home without causing it to be busy or over decorated. Since Thanksgiving two weeks ago, she'd cherished every moment that they had spent together, but it was time for her to go. He never mentioned anything beyond the moment when they were together, nothing about the future, and she was still broken. Kade deserved better, needed more than she could give him.

She'd seen Devi's colleague, Dr. Miller, as a patient once a week for the last two weeks and had visited Devi and her family informally as a friend several times. She was slowly realizing just how brainwashed she'd become from her upbringing and her marriage. Even after she'd left her foster home and her marriage to Ravi, that programming had never left her brain. It took a conscious effort every day to reprogram her thinking, to realize that she was a strong woman who deserved so much more. It wasn't going to happen overnight, but Asha liked to think she'd made a little progress.

After updating her website and posting her new phone number, she'd gotten tons of calls for new jobs, the large majority of them in Florida. No doubt it had something to do with news of her being Max and Maddie's sister, but her calendar was becoming booked, and she'd accepted all the jobs in Florida. Now that she had the funds, she wanted to get a place to plant her feet, collect things and stop running.

Her soul was completely shattered, and walking away from Kade was going to be the hardest thing she'd ever had to do—probably the hardest thing she would ever have to do—but she knew she had to do it. Maybe someday the pieces of her soul would slowly fall back into place and become whole again. Right now, the pieces were so small she couldn't see a single particle of it. There was just a black emptiness that was already haunting her, and she hadn't even left Kade's home yet.

"What are you doing?" a smooth baritone asked from the doorway.

Asha swung around, her heart leaping to her throat as she saw Kade, one hip propped against her door, his arms folded, and a puzzled look on his face. All he was wearing was a pair of jeans that rode low on his hips, leaving his incredible upper body bare. He looked freshly showered, his hair wet and sexily mussed. "Nothing...I was just getting my things together. I'm done with your house. There are no walls left for me to paint." She averted her eyes, unable to watch him move across the room without wanting to throw herself in his arms.

"So you're just planning on leaving. Just like that? Why?" he demanded, his arms encircling her waist as he stopped behind her.

Because I love you so much that I can't bear it.

Because I'm afraid if I don't leave now, I'll lose any shred of dignity that I have left after my past.

Because I need you to love me back.

Asha stepped away from him, heading for the door. "I was going to make some breakfast," she told him casually, ignoring his question.

Kade caught her as she got to the door. Backing her up against the wall, he pinned her there with his body. "Why?" he growled angrily. "Is this about the infertility thing? Dammit…talk to me. I'll tell you a secret: I've never been sure that I wanted a child of my own. My father was a fucking lunatic and my gene pool sucks. I could just as easily adopt. Having a child with my DNA isn't that important to me. Hell, I've never even really thought that seriously about having a kid, yet. I doubt I'd even make a decent father."

Asha froze, stunned. Her gaze shot to Kade's fierce expression, his eyes flashing blue fire. It didn't change anything, but his vehemence shocked her. She knew he meant what he said, that he didn't need a child with his own DNA, but it still surprised her. "Kade…I'm not helpless anymore. And I'm not broke. I can survive okay."

He entwined his fingers with hers and lifted her hands over her head, pressing his hard body into hers. Asha could feel his hard length straining against the denim of his jeans as it made contact with her pelvis. The thought of having him inside her made her choke down a moan. He held her completely captive as his tongue trailed hotly down the sensitive skin of her neck, nipping and stroking her earlobe. "I don't want you to be broke or helpless," he hissed harshly, his hot breath wafting over her ear, making her shiver with need. "I just want you to be mine."

Asha's whole body melted against him, because she *wanted* to be his. Dear God, she had no defenses when it came to this man. He made her body feel exquisite pleasures that it had never experienced before, and she greedily wanted more. Her head fell back against the wall, giving him free access to whatever he wanted. "Kade," she moaned, unable to think, unable to do anything except feel.

"That's it, baby. Moan my name. Remember how it feels to come apart for me," Kade said fiercely, untwining his fingers from hers to tear off her shirt and work the button and zipper of her jeans. "Fuck! You aren't leaving me. Not ever. Are you trying to kill me, Asha? Because you *will* kill me if you leave. I'll be so goddamn empty that I won't give a shit about anything anymore."

Asha whimpered as Kade jerked her jeans and panties from her legs and quickly lowered his own, allowing his hard length to spring free. "Fuck me, Kade. I need you." Asha needed to feel him inside her right now.

Just one more time. I need him.

He reached between her thighs, his fingers rough as they speared through her folds, her humid flesh yielding for him easily. "Tell me you won't leave," he insisted, pinching her clit just hard enough to send waves of sensation through her entire body. "Tell me you need me as much as I need you."

"I can't. I have to go. This is so good. But we have to have more than this. It's confusing," Asha panted, her arms coming around Kade's neck, pulling their flesh as tightly together as possible, the knowledge that she'd never be with him again making her desire that much more urgent. Her nipples abraded his chest; her body was primed for him, needing him.

Kade stroked her sensitive flesh roughly, and without his usual finesse. Asha had never seen him so raw and intense. He usually took his time, fanning the flames of her passion until she was mindless. But now, she was already without functioning brain cells, and she was operating on primal instinct, reacting to Kade's base need. Desperate, she snaked her legs around his waist, but it only made it easier for him to torture her. She was open to him now, and he took advantage of it, moving his fingers in and out of her pussy, abrading her clit coarsely.

"Tell me," he said in a clipped, insistent voice.

His forcefulness was ramping up her desire to new heights. Kade had always had more than his fair share of testosterone, but now he was like an alpha male completely unleashed. Kade was never going to hurt her, but this was carnal and erotic, a new dimension to his lovemaking that had her wanting even more.

"No," she cried, defying him on purpose, even though she knew she still couldn't say yes to staying with him.

"Here's a warning, sweetheart. Sometimes I like it rough and you're pushing my buttons." His voice was a low, guttural warning.

"Good," she answered, digging her nails into his back and flexing her hips against his hand between her legs. "I'm not afraid of you. Take me hard. I want you to."

"Tell me you'll stay with me." He pinched her clit between his thumb and forefinger, varying the pressure on the throbbing bundle of nerves, stroking it like a mini penis. "You've been mine since the minute I saw you. Make it official. Tell me you need me as much as I fucking need you."

"Oh, God," Asha moaned, lowering her mouth to Kade's shoulder and nipping his skin, trying to coax him to push her over the edge. "Yes," she whispered agonizingly. It was a murmur of pleasure and not an affirmative answer to Kade's demand.

"Good enough for me," Kade answered abruptly, giving her the pressure she needed, the rough caress that sent her careening over the edge.

His mouth took hers as she came apart in his arms, swallowing her screams of ecstasy, taking them into his own body as though he owned them. His tongue conquered and devoured her mouth as she shuddered in his arms.

Kade put his hands under her ass, positioned her, and plunged deep inside her. Yanking his lips from hers, he groaned, "Hold on to me, Asha. Ride me."

He had her up against the wall, and his cock began to hammer into her with volatile strokes. Asha fisted her hands in his hair and rode the waves of pleasure coursing through her body. She was pinned to the wall, his cock pummeling into her so fast she could barely take a breath. It was an elemental and primal coupling, a fierce joining of their bodies that had her body imploding and shaking with desperate need. "Yes, yes, yes," she chanted with each masterful invasion of his cock, feeling like she was being claimed. This was what she had wanted, what she had needed. Strangely enough, in this wild possession of her, he was setting her free. His savage desire for her made her feel wanted, needed and it was like a very potent aphrodisiac to her.

Bold and powerful, Kade pounded into her forcefully, groaning as Asha began to convulse around him. Relentlessly, he kept pumping his hips, drawing the pleasure to a violent crescendo.

"Holy fuck!" Kade stepped backward, letting himself collapse on the bed with Asha on top of him. They recovered their breath silently, only the sound of their pants and gasps filling the room for several minutes, before he lifted her head and looked into her eyes. "Tell me we don't belong together. I want to hear you say it if you believe it."

Asha nearly drowned in his liquid blue eyes, unable to lie. "I can't tell you that." Honestly, she didn't know for sure that she didn't belong with Kade, but she was uncertain about his feelings and confused about her own. Was it the incredible sex that made her believe that she really loved him? And she wasn't certain that the sex wasn't swaying him into believing he needed her. Was this all just a crazy love born of lust? She'd never known love, and if the love she felt for Kade was real, it was one-sided. She'd be destined to crash and burn when the glow of the earth-shattering sex wore off.

"Then how could you even think about leaving me?" Kade asked gutturally.

Disconnecting herself from Kade, Asha slid to his side. "You never asked me to stay," she murmured quietly. *And you never said how long you wanted me here, or that you loved me.*

Kade kicked his jeans completely off and rolled, pinning her beneath him. "Then I'm asking. I'm asking right now. Stay now because you want to, not because you have to. I know you have the resources to leave, but stay anyway because it's what you want."

Asha stared at his handsome face above her. He looked a little bit wild, but vulnerable too. Her heart clenched, realizing that he thought she was leaving him now that she now had money to help her along. Did he think that was the only reason she had been with him, that she had only used him?

"Goddammit, Asha! Haven't you figured out yet that you're more than a guest?" Kade grumbled.

"Then what am I?" she asked curiously, searching his face.

Your friend?

Your lover?

Girlfriend? Asha knew that one was a stretch, but Kade wasn't a guy who talked a whole lot about the future or his emotions.

"You're my fucking sanity," Kade rumbled above her. "You're the reason I stopped escaping into the pain pills I was taking."

Asha let out a tremulous breath, staring at Kade in surprise. "I thought you stopped before we met."

"I did. I stopped as soon as I started searching for you. I couldn't afford for my senses to be dulled. I needed to be in reality. You were smart. You challenged me, even though I didn't know at the time that you were running because you were scared."

"But the challenge is over," Asha answered, confused.

"Hardly," Kade answered drily. "You challenge me every single day. Watching the woman you are—all the energy and joy you put into every project you do and give to every person you meet—makes me want to be a better man."

Putting her palm against the side of his face and letting it stroke down to his whiskered jaw, she said adamantly, "You're already good." Kade was starting to find purpose in his life without her, and he was mistaken in thinking she had anything to do with his inherent decentness. It was just...him. And she had no doubt that she had very little to do with Kade's return to reality. He was strong, stubborn, and determined. He might have used pain meds as a temporary escape, but he would have broken free of them in his own time.

"I guess we just found another thing I'm good at vertically," Kade said huskily, and with a wicked grin. "Did I hurt you?" he asked anxiously.

Kade was blowing off serious emotional issues again, but Asha couldn't help but smile. "No. It was incredible."

"So you like to get a little down and dirty once in a while. Who would have imagined?" Kade answered in a pseudo shocked voice. Rolling to his back, he brought her back on top of him, palming her naked ass to keep her there.

Asha sighed, the feel of them skin-to-skin making her want to purr like a contented kitten. "A little?" she questioned skeptically.

"Sweetheart, there's a lot further down and a lot more dirty than what we just did," Kade said in a graveled voice.

"There is?" Asha couldn't keep the tinge of excitement from her voice. "Maybe I need to get some books or instructional DVDs. I think I must have missed a lot of my sex education. I've never even seen the Kama Sutra," she said teasingly.

Kade squeezed her ass cheeks, pulling her completely over him. "No need. I've read it. I'd be more than happy to corrupt and instruct you, Ms. Paritala. You've been far too good."

Matching his buoyant mood, she replied cheekily, "I have to be good or Santa will give me coal in my stocking."

"Has he done that before?" Kade asked pensively.

"I've never had a stocking before," Asha answered honestly. "I've never actually celebrated Christmas. And this was the first Thanksgiving I've ever celebrated. We only acknowledged Indian holidays, and I didn't really participate in my foster family's celebrations."

"No, you wouldn't have, would you?" Kade barked angrily. "You were their fucking servant."

Asha couldn't deny it. She was just grateful for her freedom. Her life was changing, and that was enough. "I'm starting new this year. I'm putting a Christmas tree and my stocking up." Christmas might be a religious holiday, and she wasn't sure what religion she really wanted to be, but she could celebrate just for the joy of the holiday.

Kade sat up abruptly and cradled her on his lap. "I'll be your Santa. Sit in my lap naked like this and tell Santa Kade everything you want. I guarantee you'll get everything you ask for and more."

Asha giggled, delighted by the sudden, playful change in his demeanor. "I'd wish for you to teach me the finer points of getting down and dirty."

Kade's eyes were shooting flames as he looked down at her. "Santa Kade rewards naughtiness," he said in a husky voice. "Feel free to misbehave."

Asha eyed him dubiously. "That's not the way it works. I may not have celebrated before, but I do live in America." Kade was adorable when he was mussed and playful, and Asha couldn't resist the lure of playing with him. She only had a short time left with him, and she wanted to have this day to remember. She could give herself at least that much. She knew she had to leave, for Kade's sake as well as her own. They both needed time and distance to figure out their feelings. And she needed to become a whole person.

"My rules. My Christmas." He grinned sinfully down at her.

"Okay, Santa. Let's start racking up those reward points," she answered in a sultry whisper.

Kade groaned as he fell backward and rolled her onto her back, looming large above her. "It's not nice to tease," he cautioned her in a graveled voice.

Asha's body heated as Kade held her helpless on the bed, looking like he wanted to devour her whole. "No teasing. Teach me," she beseeched, her body aching for him.

I want to experience it all today...with you.

"It could take awhile," he warned, lowering his mouth to hers. "You're still pretty innocent."

Kade's kiss took her breath away, but Asha didn't complain. Finding out just how naughty Kade could be was worth every breathless pant that came from her mouth as Kade took her to paradise.

Chapter 11

Asha left the next day. While Kade was gone to work, she put the rest of her things together and walked out the door. It was one of the hardest things she'd ever done, but she pushed herself out the door with her small suitcase, skirting Kade's security, and entered the waiting cab. Tears streamed down her face as the cab pulled away from the curb, but she knew she was doing the right thing. Her emotions were raw, and her confusion was rampant.

She and Kade had incredible sex, and she was grateful to him, but she didn't know if what they felt was love or lust. Both of them were in vulnerable positions and mutual need just wasn't going to be enough for either of them.

She'd already rented a tiny apartment across town. Although she had funds, she wanted to be careful. Still needing to purchase a car and more furnishings for the apartment, she had to be cautious with her money. Eventually, she'd contact Maddie and Max. But not yet, not when her emotions were still so fragile and not before she'd learned to truly survive alone.

This is going to hurt Kade.

The tears flowed faster and she swiped them away with impatient fingers. A short, temporary hurt was better than wounding him more in the future.

I'm still damaged.

I'm confused.

I'm not ready or worthy of a man like Kade.

Oh, but she wanted to be, and she wanted it desperately right now. The last thing she wanted was to leave him, but she cared too much about him to let him be stuck with half a woman, a woman who really didn't know who she was or what she wanted.

I start that journey of discovery today!

And there was one thing that Asha wanted, something she'd never had.

After asking the taxi driver to make a quick stop for her, she hopped out of the cab and ducked into a jewelry store. The price of gold wasn't cheap, but she bought the matching set of bangle bracelets anyway, putting a small dent in her savings.

Back in the cab, she fingered the bracelets, loving the sound of the thin hoops tinkling together. Indian women loved their bangles, and she was no different. When she was younger, she had yearned for even a cheap pair of bangles, but she'd never gotten them. Her foster parents barely fed her, and her husband never felt she deserved to have them because she couldn't get pregnant and wasn't really a woman.

Dr. Miller and Devi had recommended that she take the things she liked and wanted from her Indian heritage and dump the bad things because she was, after all, an American. And one thing she'd always coveted was bangles. Maybe it was imbedded in her DNA, but she'd always wanted them. She'd been deprived of the right to wear them even though she had been raised as an Indian woman. Now, she could decide what she wanted for herself. That thought both soothed and terrified her. She'd gone from a demanding, controlling foster family to an abusive husband. Even the last two years had been decisions made only for survival.

Who am I?

What do I want?

Her errant thoughts were interrupted as she arrived at her apartment building. After hastily paying and tipping the driver, she exited the cab and strode toward her apartment, nervous and apprehensive, but feeling stronger than she'd ever felt in her entire life.

I wish I could tell Kade how I feel.

Chastising herself for the thought, she realized that it was going to take a long time *not* to miss Kade. In addition to being an incredible lover, he had become her first true friend, the one man who had treated her with respect and kindness. He was special, and deep in her heart, Asha knew it. But he was more than a friend, and staying in his life would just make everything murky and confused. Maybe leaving his home had partially been for her protection, too. She believed Kade deserved more than a confused, messed-up woman, but she was fighting emotions that she just couldn't deal with right at the moment. Kade overwhelmed her, and she wasn't strong enough yet to deal with those intense feelings.

Letting herself into the apartment, she closed the door and locked it behind her.

"Home sweet home," she said to herself, looking around the sparsely furnished apartment. She had a couch and a bed, along with a few bare essentials, but she needed to shop for the rest of what she needed. She'd rented the apartment a few days ago and Devi's family had helped her move the few things she had purchased into the apartment. Now, it was time to make it a home for herself.

She propped her suitcase against the couch and studied the bare, white walls. One of the first things she needed was paint. She was Indian, and she needed color. She'd paint over the decorations before she left someday so she didn't annoy the landlord, but the walls were depressing.

I have jobs starting the day after tomorrow. Time to get to work.

She took her bag to her bedroom, opening it to find the computer that Kade had given her on the very top. Tears sprang to her eyes, and she felt the enormous waves of loneliness that threatened to crush her.

Do this for him. Don't let his kindness be for nothing.

Succeed! Succeed! Succeed!

In that moment, Asha found a new mantra, and she was determined to keep it.

"You did an incredible job with Holderman," Travis commented casually as he plopped into the chair in front of Kade's desk in his office at Harrison. "A hell of a lot better than I could have managed."

Kade shrugged. "He's an ass, but we want the acquisition."

"I'm not sure I would have pursued it. The company would have lost money because I don't have the patience to deal with him," Travis replied, straightening his tie, obviously wanting to say something, but looking like he was reluctant or unable to say it.

"So you needed me," Kade said jokingly. More seriously, he added, "It was no big deal. I've had to deal with a lot of assholes in my life. I've learned not to let them get to me. Winning the game is more important."

"I'm glad you're here, Kade. I just wanted you to know that," Travis grumbled, looking a little uncomfortable. "You have strengths that I don't, and we complement each other."

Kade looked at his twin in surprise. "Who are you and what have you done with my brother?" The comment was so unlike Travis that Kade wasn't quite sure he'd heard Travis properly. His twin didn't admit to having any weaknesses.

"I'm just stating a fact. Harrison is better for having you here." Travis shifted in his chair, straightening his already perfect tie. "I just wish you'd rethink your shirts and ties."

Kade barked out a laugh. *That* comment was more like Travis, but he was touched that Travis wanted him here. "I thought you had everything under control. I never felt like you needed me."

"I don't," Travis said defensively. "If you want to do something else with your life, you can feel free to leave Harrison to me."

Kade studied Travis, trying to read him, but it was almost impossible. Luckily, they were twins, and Kade sensed certain things about his brother. Right now, Travis was trying to set him free to do whatever he wanted to do because his elder brother had always taken up all the responsibilities at Harrison, allowing the rest of the siblings to pursue their dreams. Kade had never thought about the sacrifices Travis had made for his family, but now he asked, "Do you like being here? Do you like running Harrison? You could have been a hell of a race car driver if you'd stayed with that. But you couldn't, could you? You were the only one left to run the company." Kade's gut twisted with guilt. "You were the only one who never felt free to do what you wanted. You were trapped here because Mia was pursuing her art and I was playing football." Kade had never thought about the unfairness of that fact until now. He'd always just assumed that Travis was exactly where he wanted to be.

"It was fair," Travis rumbled. "I wasn't deprived. I was doing exactly what I wanted. I like racing, but it's a hobby. I never felt the driving need to do it professionally. I wanted to be here. So don't try to make me out to be some type of hero. I love this company and the way it challenges me."

You like the way it takes up all your time and helps you forget. Kade knew that Travis buried himself in his work. But he was relieved that he hadn't had a burning desire to do something else. "I want to be here, Travis. I just felt like you didn't need me here because you had it all handled, had it all together."

"I do," Travis drawled arrogantly. "But I could use your help."

Kade stifled a chuckle, knowing that he wasn't going to get any more than that admission from Travis. But it was good enough for him. Admittedly, he felt needed here. Slowly, the duties that were weaknesses for Travis had been passed to him, and he found that he truly did excel at the things that Travis didn't. The employees were starting to look to him for guidance in those areas, and he was starting to feel like the captain of his own football team. "I'm here. And I'm not going anywhere."

"Good," Travis answered briskly, standing and brushing imaginary wrinkles from his suit.

"But I'm not changing the way I dress unless it's for a necessary function that requires I be boring," Kade warned him, trying to keep the laughter from his voice.

"Agreed," Travis replied reluctantly. Stopping with his hand on the doorknob and his back to Kade, he paused. "You know, sometimes it scares the hell out of me, but I'm actually starting to look forward to seeing your fluffy bunny shirts and dancing banana ties every day."

"Well, damn," Kade said under his breath. "I guess he did miss me." His brother's comment was the closest thing he'd ever heard to a confession that he wanted to be closer to Kade, see him more often.

Travis moved to leave, but turned around again. "Incidentally, we've uncovered some not-so-legal business practices of Asha's ex-husband. He employs Indian students illegally and works them like dogs. Pays them almost nothing, but they're desperate so they do it. Since they aren't supposed to be working here on a student visa, they keep their mouths shut about it. Rumor has it that the women get the worst of it, but they can't report him when he mistreats them or assaults them because they're afraid they'll be in trouble for working illegally."

"Bastard," Kade spat out with disgust.

"He'll get what's coming to him, Kade. Be patient. This will help more people than just Asha," Travis said cautiously, drilling Kade with an intense stare.

Kade shook his head, trying to push down on the anger he felt every time he imagined someone hurting Asha. But now that he knew the asshole was hurting others, he knew he had to find a way to control himself. After all, Asha was safe. "I'll wait," he answered in a clipped voice.

Travis's phone started blasting an upbeat music ringtone, and he yanked the phone from his pocket, glaring at it like it was his worst enemy. "Goddamn it! How the hell did she get my phone this time?"

"Ms. Caldwell?" Kade asked, smirking at Travis's phone.

"She's a pain in my ass. She's fired this time." Travis stomped out of the office, the door closing behind him.

Kade chuckled, staring at the closed door, not the least bit afraid for Ally. Travis threatened to fire her at least once a day, and she was still here. His brother could snarl and get pissed off all he wanted…there was no way he'd get rid of Ally. He needed her too much. Honestly, Kade wasn't sure what Travis would do without her anymore. She might irritate the hell out of him, but she kept him on his toes.

Glancing at the clock, he decided it was time to go home.

As he left the office, he grinned at his secretary, Karen, and she smiled right back, both of them hearing the heated exchange between Ally and Travis in the next office. Kade doubted anyone took it seriously anymore because it happened on a daily basis.

"Have a good night, Mr. Harrison," Karen chirped.

"You, too," he returned with a wave.

Every night had been good lately now that he had Asha. He didn't expect tonight to be any different.

He drove home way faster than he should, anxious to get to his house and see Asha's smiling face, wondering how he'd gotten so dependent on seeing her in such a short space of time. But he had, and having her in his life had changed the way he looked at everything now. His future was no longer bleak, and he was moving on with his life. Finally, he was starting to think less and less about the football career he had lost and more about what lay ahead in the future. He parked in front of his house with a smile on his face.

Kade was assaulted by the feeling of emptiness the moment he entered his house.

Asha's not here.

It was odd, but he could always sense her presence. There was a feeling of lightness and joy in his home whenever Asha was present. When she wasn't, it was vacant and oppressively lonely.

"Asha?" He called her name urgently as he checked the kitchen, only to find it empty. He bolted up the stairs, shedding his suit jacket as he went.

He immediately noticed the two large drawings on the bed, and he moved closer to study them.

The first drawing was one he recognized. It was the self-portrait that he had seen when he'd first taken Asha's things, the picture of her yearning for a man, and the man's face in shadow. Moving on to the next, he recognized himself right away, and he identified Asha as the woman with her head resting against his shoulder. A woman who appeared incredibly happy and satisfied.

Two pictures.

Both subjects the same.

But the emotions were completely different.

Holding them up, Kade looked at them side by side. He understood her message immediately. He'd have to be a complete idiot not to comprehend that she was telling him that he'd satisfied her needs. He replaced the pictures, his heart thundering in his chest, happy beyond belief that Asha was saying he'd made her happy. 'Cause really, that was all he wanted.

There was a note next to the pictures, and he picked it up and opened it. There was only one paragraph:

Dearest Kade,

I wanted to say good-bye in person, but I guess I'm a coward. Maybe that's one of the many things I need to work on about myself. I couldn't go without thanking you for everything you've done for me. You saved my life, but I can't stay. I'm not strong enough for this right now, and I'm confused. I need time and space to work on my problems. You don't deserve a woman as messed-up and broken as I am right now. Please forgive me for not telling you this in person, but I think it's better this way. I called the hospital in Nashville to get the total of the bill. My work doesn't cover the full amount, so I've left a check for the rest on your dresser. You'll never know how much I cherish our time together, and I'll never forget everything you've done for me.

Be Happy,

Asha

Kade walked to his dresser in a daze, unable to process what Asha had written. He picked up the check, absently noting that she needed to charge more for her work. It was nearly the full amount of her hospital bill. Next to the check was the phone he'd given her, and the reason that she had left it was obvious.

She wants to make sure I can't contact her.

"She can't really be gone," he assured himself in a disbelieving voice.

Walking into the room across the hall, he found the clothing that Maddie and Mia had bought her. The room looked the same, but it felt different. The laptop he had gifted her was gone from the desk. The dresser drawers where she kept the clothes she wore were empty, and her suitcase was gone.

"No," he denied emphatically, shaking his head as he stared blankly at the empty drawer he'd just opened. "She wouldn't leave me. She said she wouldn't."

Ultimately, reality crept in, leaving him rooted to the carpet on the floor of her room, his whole body shuddering.

His disbelief turned to frustration and disappointment...and finally desolation. "Why? Why would she go?" he rasped, already knowing what the answer was to his question. She simply didn't want to be with *him*.

His fist crashed down on the dresser hard enough to make a mark. "Fuck! Did I really think she'd be happy with me?" he shouted loudly, devastation eating at his soul. "I'm a lame bastard with nothing to offer except money, and she doesn't need that anymore." Completely destroyed, he kicked out with his damaged leg, slamming it into the dresser. It hurt like hell, but the agony of losing Asha was still more acute, a fiery pain in his chest that threatened to consume him.

Limping to the bed, he sat, staring at the picture Asha had painted on this accent wall. It was a beach scene, waves crashing to the shore and a sky that seemed to stretch to infinity. Right now, Kade wished he could be in the drawing, let it swallow him up and devour him.

You can't let this destroy you.

He tried reaching inside himself for some last reserve of strength or endurance, but he found none. There was nothing left.

Kade slept in Asha's bed that night, the light smell of jasmine torturing him until it slowly faded away, taking any glimmer of happiness he'd had along with it.

Chapter 12

The first six weeks of Asha's total freedom turned out to be one of the most difficult times of her life. Not talking to Kade, not seeing his handsome face every day was agony, and the desire to call him was almost irresistible. She picked up her new phone several times a day, only to shove it back in her purse again with a sigh. Those ties were broken, and chances were that she wouldn't get a positive reaction from him. She'd burnt that bridge in an effort to give Kade a chance to find a better partner, and she needed to stay out of his life.

Finally, she'd admitted to herself that she hadn't really been confused about the way she felt about him. She loved him. Probably always would. Most of her fears arose from the uncertainty of how he felt about her, and her certainty that he deserved a much better woman in his life than her.

Christmas came and went, and she had put up a tree, but she decided against the stocking. It would end up as empty as her life on Christmas morning.

She continued her therapy with Dr. Miller, trying to free herself from the invisible chains that had held her immobile her entire life. She worked nearly every day, and had bought a used compact car to get around. Driving was a challenge. Although she had a license, she had driven very little in her life. She cursed other drivers often, but she was a little afraid that it was really her skills that were lacking.

However, every day she grew more confident in everything new that she was doing, and started losing her fear of life. Sometimes trying to shed the guilt and shame that plagued her seemed like an uphill battle, but she kept taking small steps up the incline. She'd get there…eventually.

"I have a small confession to make," her neighbor, Tate Colter, told her as he poured himself another cup of coffee.

His voice jolted her out of her musings. Tate had been a glimmer of light for Asha. She'd met him a week after she'd moved into her apartment. He lived directly across the hall, and on the day he'd moved in, they had literally bumped into each other. She was getting into the elevator as Tate was getting out. He was on crutches from a broken leg, but she'd failed to see him because she was in a hurry and had literally bowled him over, leaving the poor guy on the floor of the elevator. Mortified, she'd helped him up and followed him to his apartment, trying to make sure she hadn't damaged his leg. He'd assured her he was fine and invited himself over for coffee.

"I'm not really gay," he admitted, his voice just a little guilty.

Asha smiled as she sipped her coffee at Tate's kitchen table. When she had hesitated that first day to invite him in, he had assured her he was no threat because he wasn't interested in women except as friends. "Really?" she questioned pseudo innocently, already having guessed the truth quite some time ago.

"You looked nervous and I didn't want to scare you. So it was the best thing I could think of at the time," Tate said, his voice remorseful. "Forgive me?"

Asha looked at him and the nearly irresistible grin he gave her. Tate was incredibly attractive. With his pleading gray eyes, short blond hair, and the hint of a dimple on the side of his smiling mouth, Asha was pretty sure there wasn't a woman in the world who wouldn't cave when they looked at him. She sighed, wishing she could be just a little bit attracted to Tate, but she wasn't. She loved his company, but she was starting to think that anyone who wasn't Kade just wouldn't do it for her. "I already did. Weeks ago."

"You guessed? What gave me away?" Tate asked curiously.

"Hmm...I think my first clue was the attractive brunette who comes in and out of your apartment. She always has a giddy, love-struck expression on her face every time I see her coming or going from your place."

Tate shrugged. "It's not serious."

Asha gave him an admonishing look. "I think she thinks that it is."

"Nah...she knows the deal," he answered, his voice detached. "She doesn't want anything serious either. She's recently divorced and is just looking for a casual thing."

Asha didn't think so, but it was really none of her business, so she didn't comment. "I guess I should get back to work." Tate was her latest client, and she needed to finish the accent wall in his apartment. "You realize you'll have to repaint over this when you move?"

"Yeah. But it's worth the effort if I can see your amazing work every day. It already looks incredible. It's getting late. You can work on it tomorrow. You look tired."

Asha was tired, and she didn't have much to do to finish Tate's project. She was doing a scene with a vintage fire truck on his wall, and it was turning out very well. Tate had given her the photos and she was creating the scene with the aid of the pictures. He had told her that he collected antiques and had a fascination for old fire trucks and fire equipment.

"Okay," she agreed, draining her coffee cup. "I have something to do in the morning. Can I come over in the afternoon to finish up?" She stood and grabbed her keys from the table.

"Yeah. No problem," he said agreeably, following her to the door. "Asha?"

"Yeah?" She turned to look at Tate.

"I'm sorry I bullshitted you. I like you, and I shouldn't have lied. I feel pretty guilty since you've gone out of your way to look after me while I've had my cast on." He moved forward and brushed his lips against her forehead in a gesture of apology.

Tate looked so sincere that Asha smiled. "I don't do anything I don't want to do anymore. You shouldn't have lied, but I understand why you did. I'm not sure I would have befriended you at the time, had you not said you were gay."

"Bad relationship?" he asked in a concerned voice.

"A few years ago, yes. My trust in men isn't all that great."

"Not all men suck," Tate answered with a grin.

"I know. I've met some good ones now," Asha answered as she opened the door.

"Am I included in that group?" Tate asked hopefully.

"Time will tell," Asha said nonchalantly. "I guess that depends on whether or not you keep stringing along that nice brunette and break her heart."

Asha heard an exaggerated groan from Tate as she closed the door and went back to her own apartment with a cheeky smile.

Asha tried to keep her nervousness under control as she pulled her vehicle to the front gate of Maddie's home, asking the security guard to let Maddie know she was here. She'd wanted to come visit her sister so many times, but she hadn't been able to bring herself to do it.

Security opened the gate for her, and Maddie met her on the steps of her house. Her older sister didn't say a word as Asha approached. Maddie simply pulled Asha into her arms and held her tightly, comfortingly. They stayed like that for a while, Asha hugging Maddie back and savoring the comfort of her sibling's embrace.

Finally, Maddie spoke in a tremulous voice, "I was afraid I wasn't going to see you again."

"I'm sorry, Maddie. I should have contacted you. I just...couldn't." Listening to her sister's concerned voice, Asha realized she should have at least called. But she wasn't used to someone caring about whether or not she was okay.

"Something happened with Kade." It was a statement from Maddie, not a question.

Asha backed slowly out of Maddie's arms and let her lead her into the kitchen. "It wasn't him. It was me. I fell in love with him. So I had to leave."

Maddie stopped at the coffee pot and poured them both some coffee before turning to Asha and raising a questioning brow. "You had to leave him because you love him?" Nodding to the cups of coffee, she mentioned, "Sorry...it's decaf. I'm banned from caffeine until the babies come."

The women sat, each with a mug of coffee in front of them. Asha added cream and sugar to hers. "I drink a lot of herbal chai, so I don't drink much caffeine either."

"I was so afraid you weren't going to contact me. The DNA test came back and was a positive match, just the way I knew it would be. We're sisters, Asha. Officially," Maddie said, her voice emotional. Tears started to flow from her eyes as she looked across the table at Asha.

Asha lowered her head. "I know. I think I've always known. I was just afraid, Maddie. I'm sorry." Seeing her sister crying nearly undid her. Maddie was upset. About her. It was more than clear that her older sister cared, and it made Asha's chest ache with longing. "I needed some time. I've never really been on my own, made my own decisions without anyone making them for me. I'm messed up, Maddie. I need to get my head on straight, learn to make my own decisions and be independent. I never meant to hurt you. I'm not used to anyone caring about me."

Maddie's face softened. "Oh, Asha. Of course people care. Max and I love you, and you have friends. I think you're going to have to get used to people caring." She hesitated before adding, "Kade loves you, too. He's been torn up since you left. He doesn't talk about it a lot, but he's not doing well. He told Max that you didn't want to be with him."

"He's not well? What's wrong with him?" Asha asked anxiously, worried that something was wrong with Kade. And his assumption that she didn't want to be with him couldn't be further from the real truth.

"Max sees him more than I do, but he says Kade is walking around in a daze, like he doesn't care about anything."

Asha took a sip of her coffee, her mind racing. "Is he still working with Travis at Harrison every day?"

Maddie nodded. "Yeah. But even Travis is worried about him, and Travis rarely talks about or shows that he's concerned, even if he is."

Asha's distress nearly made her get up and run to Kade to see if he was okay, but would Kade even want to see her? Right now, she didn't know. Was he really mourning her loss that much? She had thought he'd get over her pretty quickly once she was gone. She wasn't exactly a prize. They'd had phenomenal sex, and his kindness made him protective of her, but was it possible that he missed her as much as she missed him? "What do you think is wrong?"

"I think he's heartbroken. First Amy left him, and now you. His recovery from the accident was long and painful. I think he's hitting an all-time low. I don't think Amy really affected anything except his pride. But he's pretty devastated about you leaving."

"I don't know what to do." Asha buried her face in her hands, unsure of what action she should take. The last thing she wanted was to see Kade suffer, but she wasn't sure that seeing him would really make the situation any better.

Maddie reached across the table and squeezed Asha's hand. "You need to take care of yourself first, Asha. Take whatever time you need to heal. You've been through way too much. You said your marriage was bad, but your ex-husband was abusive, wasn't he?"

"Very," she blurted out. The floodgates opened and she started to tell Maddie the whole truth about her upbringing and her marriage, not able to stop until the whole story was out. She didn't want to put distance between herself and her siblings anymore, and she wanted Maddie to know the truth. It wasn't a dirty little secret she needed to hide. For once, she was beginning to realize that it wasn't her fault.

"Oh my God. I'm so sorry," Maddie said sadly, after Asha had unburdened herself about the trials of her marriage.

"Don't be," Asha answered. "It wasn't your fault. And I'm lucky I got out. I guess it's hard to understand how the Indian culture is so motivated by shame and guilt. Knowing how and who my father was, I wish I had rebelled and never married. I wish I had handled everything differently. It never even occurred to me to do anything differently until I realized I really didn't want to die."

"It's not the only culture where women are abused, Asha. It may be much more frequent and acceptable in Indian culture, but American women stay in abusive relationships, get mired in the cycle of abuse. Once you're in the cycle, it's very hard to get out. I'm just glad you're escaping. Please know that Max and I will help you. We're here for you. Are you getting counseling?"

"Yes. I'm seeing one of Devi's colleagues. But I know I have to be responsible for making the changes myself. Dr. Miller opens my eyes to reality, and I'm doing my best to change myself." Asha paused before adding, "I have a little apartment, and my business is thriving. I'm doing good, Maddie."

"But you miss Kade?" Maddie questioned softly.

"So much it hurts," Asha admitted to her sister. "I'm in love with him. At first, I wondered if I was confusing love with lust. The sex was incredible. But I miss everything about him. I think I'm realizing that the sex was incredible because I do love him."

"And because he loves you?" Maddie questioned.

"Men are different," Asha said morosely, thinking about Tate's circumstances with the brunette. "I think they can have good sex without having their feelings involved."

Maddie laughed. "True. But not *that* good."

Asha looked at Maddie, her heart in her eyes. "What should I do?"

"That's for you to decide. You *are* making your own decisions now," Maddie told her warmly.

"Yeah. I guess I am," Asha answered with a small smile. "It's hard to get used to."

"You'll get used to it. I'm so proud of you, Asha. It takes a strong woman to survive what you've been through and then take charge of her life." Maddie looked at her fondly.

Asha's heart swelled. No one had ever been proud of her. "Thanks. I'm still a work in progress."

"We all are." Maddie took a sip of her coffee and set it down on the table. "None of us are without our issues. But admitting you have them and wanting to change things is the biggest step."

"Thanks for supporting me," Asha told her sincerely. "I'm so happy to have such an amazing woman for a sister."

"Thanks for letting me support you," Maddie quickly replied. "Max will be there for you, too."

"Thank you, Maddie." Asha rose and went to hug her sister, realizing how much knowing that she had her support added to her resolve. "I have to go. I have a project this afternoon."

Maddie got up and wrapped her arm around Asha. "I'm off today. Sam is so anxious, and I don't like seeing him stressed out. I'm only working part-time until the babies come. Maybe we can spend some time together. Please don't shut me out. I want to help, even if you just need someone to listen."

Asha made plans to see Maddie later in the week, wishing she had come to her earlier. Truth was, it had been selfish of her. Maddie wanted to support her independence, but Asha knew she would hurt every time she saw anyone who reminded her of Kade.

Start realizing that people care—and nurture that affection.

In other words, she needed to get used to it and accept it as truth. People cared about her now, and she needed to be careful of their feelings. Before, her actions had never really affected anyone. Now they did, and she had the ability to hurt people who cared about her.

She left Maddie's home and thought about *that* nearly unbelievable truth all the way home.

sha visited Max the next morning, hoping he wasn't working because it was a Saturday. She parked her car in front of his house, and hesitantly approached the security at his front gate, pulling her driver's license out of her purse.

"Go on in," the burly security agent told her when she handed him her license. "We've been instructed by Mr. and Mrs. Hamilton that you're to be admitted immediately any time you visit. You're family. All of us will recognize your face eventually," the guard continued, flashing a shy smile at her as she passed through the gate.

I'm family. I really do have a sister and a brother.

Asha smiled back at the man, still trying to wrap her head around his comment. Would she ever get used to being related to Maddie and Max?

"Looks like your tire is almost flat, Ms. Paritala," the guard called to her from the gate as she made her way up to the house.

Waving to acknowledge that she heard the guard, she made a note to ask Max if he had anyone who could help her change her tire. She'd known the vehicle needed new tires, but she hadn't gotten replacements put on yet. The price had been right on the small, used compact, even with necessity of buying new tires.

Max lived right on the beach, the sound of the waves and the smell of salt water assaulting her senses. She'd actually never been inside his residence, but she had passed by the area before with Kade, and he had pointed out Max's place. It was hard to believe any member of her family lived in such an opulent residence.

Maybe visiting Max and Maddie so close together had been a bad idea. Just seeing how successful her siblings were two days in a row was intimidating. But she really needed to see Max. After seeing how upset Maddie was that she hadn't contacted her, she wanted to make sure she saw Max, too.

Asha hit the doorbell with a sigh, trying to compartmentalize her thoughts, trying to think of Max as her brother instead of as a billionaire. Strange, but she had never really been intimidated by Kade's billionaire status.

Probably because I was too busy admiring his other assets!

Kade overwhelmed her as a man, so his wealth had never really been something she concerned herself with that often. He had kept her too dizzy with pleasure and desire to think about his money or status.

"Asha," Mia said in a surprised but happy voice as she pulled open the door, a fleeting expression of worry crossing her face before it turned into a genuine smile. She pulled her into an enthusiastic hug on the doorstep, holding Asha tightly as she added, "We were worried about you."

Asha hugged Mia back, loving the comforting feeling of her embrace. "I'm sorry. I got myself a place. A little apartment," she said, trying to make everything sound like she was doing well.

Mia pulled back and smiled at her. "I know. Max kept tabs on you. We knew you were safe."

"You knew where I was?" she asked, entering the house as Mia held the door open for her.

"Of course. You didn't think Max would let his sister disappear and not know where she was living, did you? But I'm glad you came. He's been worried about you."

"How did he find out where I was living?" Really, her brother's capabilities and power were a little bit scary.

Mia lifted a brow at her. "He found you when he didn't know anything about you. It was easier this time."

Asha supposed she should be upset that her brother was spying on her, but he had been looking out for her, worried about her. And she hadn't contacted him. She couldn't possibly chastise him for caring. "I was going to contact you. I wanted to. I just needed some time."

"Maddie called me last night. I understand," Mia told Asha reassuringly. "Are you okay?"

She nodded at her slowly. "Yeah. I'm good. My business is really busy and I enrolled in some art classes."

Asha stopped in the doorway of the den Mia was leading her toward, hearing voices that sounded familiar. "You have company?" she asked Mia, concerned that she'd interrupted a visit from someone else.

She could hear Max's furious voice, but couldn't make out exactly what he was saying.

"Asha…your foster parents are here," Mia answered, sounding tense and frustrated.

That was why the tone of the voices had sounded familiar. "W-why?" she stammered. "Why would they come here?"

"They're looking for you," Mia answered bluntly. "Somehow they got the news in California that you're a sibling to Max and Maddie. They wanted to talk to you. I think Max is ripping them a new asshole right now."

Asha's world tilted and rocked for just a moment before becoming upright again. For just a few moments, she was an adolescent again, terrified of displeasing her foster parents, and losing the only home she had. "Is my ex-husband with them?"

"No. If he was, he wouldn't still be able to speak. Max would have killed him by now," Mia said fiercely. "Max let your foster parents in just so he could tell them what he thought about the way they fostered you. They'll be shown out shortly."

Mia wrapped her arms around her midsection, rocking a little in distress. "I don't know what they want from me," she answered, her voice radiating with vulnerability.

"Nothing good," Mia replied, waving Asha into the den.

Asha knew this was a pivotal moment for her, a short period of time where she could take the easy way out by avoiding her foster parents, or confront her demons. She could run and hide...or deal with them herself. She wasn't a child anymore...she was an adult. Really, it wasn't something that Max should have to contend with and he didn't need to.

"I'll talk to them," she told Mia, looking into her sister-in-law's concerned face with a determined expression. "I don't need to be afraid of them anymore and I don't need to be obedient. I want them out of your house and gone, and I don't want them to bother you and Max again."

She turned on her heel and followed the voices, which wasn't difficult since Max was bellowing at the top of his lungs. "Are you fucking kidding me? It wasn't Asha who complained; it was me. Neither one of you is fit to be a foster parent and you'll never foster another child."

Asha stopped in the entryway to the living room, stunned. Max had filed a complaint? On her behalf?

Mia stopped her with a hand on her shoulder, whispering next to her ear. "It wasn't just you, Asha. After you left, they took in another foster child of around ten years old. They're getting ready to marry her off to another one of their relatives in India—for a very hefty price. And they just applied for another one. Another female. Max blocked their application with a complaint. This might get unpleasant."

"They did it again?" Asha asked incredulously, anger rising up from her belly, anger for the girl who was about to marry a man she most probably didn't want to wed. "We have to stop the marriage unless she wants it."

"Max already did. She didn't want it, but was in the same circumstances as you were at the time. She wants to go to college to be a teacher. Max already has her at the school and settled into her dorm. We're helping her. Don't worry. And Max will make certain they never get another foster child again."

Tears of anger and relief flooded Asha's eyes. "Thank you," she whispered fiercely. "You have no idea how much this will change her life." Although the teenager had probably grown up mired in the same guilt and shame as Asha, the course of her life had changed because of Mia and Max.

Mia squeezed her hand and Asha turned to face her foster parents, who were still arguing with Max. Letting go of Mia's hand, she lifted her chin and walked into the room. All conversation stopped as she approached her foster parents, every eye on her.

"You will leave my brother's house and never come near any of my family again," Asha told her foster parents abruptly, her anger still boiling inside her.

Her foster mother stepped forward, gold bangles clinking as she moved. She looked very much the same, but different to Asha now that she was seeing her through the eyes of an adult. Her eyes moved over the finest silk sari that her foster mother was wearing, and the gold and gems that adorned her body. Why had she ever believed that her foster parents were suffering financially? Her foster mother was wearing enough to gold to live off for life.

I was a servant, and then I was sold, just like Kade told me I was. There were no financial difficulties, no reason for what they did except profit.

"What? You no longer speak Telugu?" her foster mother admonished.

"I'm American, and I live in America. I speak English. My brother and his wife speak English. I wouldn't be that rude to speak in a language they don't speak," she answered angrily.

"How dare you? We fed you, we raised you, and you talk back to my wife?" her foster father answered furiously.

"You took me in and sold me off. In the meantime, I was an unpaid servant to you. You even sold my father's things," Asha answered bravely, stepping forward to get in her foster father's face. "How dare *you?"* Taking a deep breath, she continued. "Did you know that Ravi abused me? Did you know what he did to me?"

"He was trying to discipline you. And he was disappointed that you never gave him a child," her foster mother answered, as though it were natural for such a thing to happen.

Asha blew out a heavy breath, getting the answer she had expected but had hoped wasn't true. They had known, and they'd let it happen. "You're both horrible people. My father worked to protect the rights of women, and you sell them like they're chattels. It has nothing to do with culture and everything to do with both of you being selfish and cruel individuals, although you need to open your eyes and see that Indian women are tired of being treated poorly, tired of being slapped around and subjected to the will of men. I wasn't able to bear a child, but that doesn't mean I deserved to be beaten because of something that wasn't my fault."

"Your father, your father..." Her foster father threw his hand in the air and let go of a snort of disgust. "He was a dreamer who died poor because of his stupid ideals."

"His karma was rich," Asha snapped back at him.

"You need to return to your husband," her foster mother said sternly. "You can help him financially now."

"Because my relatives are rich, you think some of their money should go to Ravi?" Asha fumed, disgusted that they really believed that she owed anything to a man who had nearly killed her on several occasions. They likely thought they would share in the riches. "I pay my own way. I don't sponge off others, or sell people to make money. And I'd die before I'd return to the prison of an abuser again."

"He's your husband," her foster father boomed.

"He's nothing to me. We're divorced, and if and when I remarry, it will be to the man of my choice."

"Whore!" Her foster father raised his arm to strike her. Asha moved quickly, ducking and scrambling backward as a large body pushed between her and her foster father. A large hand came up lightning fast to manacle her foster father's wrist as it swung. Asha lost her balance, her momentum carrying her backward and onto her ass in the middle of the carpet.

"She dishonors her husband. She's a tramp," her foster mother wailed.

Max came forward and looked at the whining woman, giving her a disgusted glance before grasping her wrist. "You're leaving. And don't say another word. I've never hit a woman before in my entire life, but lady, you're the first who's made me even wish that I could."

Asha looked up, a little dazed, first at Max tugging on her foster mother, and then at her foster father, who was being restrained by someone who made her heart accelerate and her breath catch.

Kade!

The two men were in profile to her, but she could see the rage on Kade's face, veins pulsating in his neck. His breathing was ragged and the glare he was giving her foster father was one of pure furious wrath. He was like a serpent the moment before it struck with deadly intent.

"We will leave. You're dead to us," her foster mother said with a sniff.

Asha thought that was nothing new. She'd always been dead to them, and if Ravi had killed her, he wouldn't have been blamed by either one of them.

Max's security swarmed the room, taking the woman from Max's grasp and leading her toward the door.

"Kade. Don't. Neither one of them is worth it," Asha said softly, trying to coax Kade out of going on a rampage. She could see his resolve, and it frightened her. She didn't want him caught up in her problems.

Asha rose quickly, and put her hand on Kade's shoulder. "Please," she whispered into his ear.

"He was going to hit you," Kade rasped, the breath sawing in and out of his lungs rapidly, as though he were losing control.

"He didn't. You saved me. Let him leave."

Her foster father stood in stony silence, trying to move by Kade to leave, but he couldn't escape Kade's grasp.

"Fine. He can go. Right after this." Kade pulled back his powerful arm and slammed his fist into the older man's face. The force was powerful enough to bring her foster father to his knees.

"You broke my nose," the older man whimpered, holding his hand to his bloody nose.

Security pushed by Kade and hauled her foster father to his feet.

Glaring at him, Kade said caustically, "Don't expect me to get you a fucking tissue. You're a damn coward, and if I had you alone for five minutes, I'd break more than your nose. If you ever get near her again, you'll deal with me."

"I thought you were some football hero," her foster father said with disgust.

"Right now, I'm just a pissed-off man. Get him the hell out of my sight," Kade told the agents who were holding the man up.

Max had his arms wrapped around Mia, and the room emptied except for them, Kade, and Asha.

"Are you okay?" Kade grumbled, rubbing his hands up and down her arms and scrutinizing her face. "Fuck! I wanted to kill the bastard, but I think you've witnessed enough violence in your life."

"I didn't see you come in," she commented softly, still trying to calm down the whole situation.

"I walked in just a few minutes before the bastard raised his hand to you."

"You're still fast," Max said, looking at Kade gratefully. "I wouldn't have made it quick enough." He left Mia's side long enough to hug Asha, whispering quietly, "I'm so proud of you. I know it wasn't easy to stand up to them. You did great."

Strangely, it wasn't all that difficult, but she blushed at Max's compliment. Maybe she was getting some gumption, or maybe she was just finally able to define the line between right and wrong. "It was past time. Thank you for helping the foster child they were planning on marrying off. I'd like to give you some money to help her."

Max drew back and shook his head. "Not happening. She's a sweet girl and she'll make a wonderful teacher. I'm happy to help her. I've already set her up with everything she needs for her education and expenses. She's fine, Asha."

"Then I want to set up an organization of some kind. To help other abused women get free. It was something I wanted to talk to you about. You're a great investor. Can you help me invest the money my father gave me so I can carry on his legacy?" she asked Max hopefully.

"Already done. The foundation has even been named after your father." It was Kade who spoke this time. "And it's well-funded at the moment."

"But I want to do something," Asha objected. "I want to give something."

"Harrison set it up and it's funded by several billionaires. But we could use your volunteer time," Max told her quietly.

"You set this up?" Asha questioned Kade, her heart thundering as she looked at him. He looked tired, dark circles marring the skin under his eyes and lines of tension showing on his face.

Kade shrugged. "We all did. Max, Travis, Sam, Simon, and I are the primary donors."

"That's incredible. I don't know how to thank you all." She looked from Mia and Max to Kade, tears of gratitude in her eyes. "But what about my funds? Won't they help?"

Max grinned at her. "We have other donors lined up. I think you need to invest it for your future."

"I'll help you," Kade grunted.

Max nodded. "You're good. Maybe better than I am," Max agreed a little grudgingly.

"I want to learn to do it myself," Asha commented stubbornly.

"I'll teach you," Kade assented. "I'll just advise while you're learning."

Asha nodded eagerly. "Thank you."

The tension between her and Kade was almost palpable, and although she wanted to see him, being near him was difficult. "I should go. I'm sure you came to visit Max." She hugged Mia and kissed Max on the cheek. "Thank you. For everything."

"We're family. I know you aren't used to having family, but get used to it. We'll be meddling in your business all the time," Max answered with an arrogance and confidence of a man who planned on being her protector for life.

Mia elbowed Max in the ribs. "But only in a good way," she rushed to add.

Asha laughed, her joy at having people who really cared about her too difficult to hold inside her. "I'll work on getting used to it," she agreed. "Oh. I forgot. Do you have anyone who can help me change my tire? I think it's flat. I have a spare, but I'm not sure I have the equipment I need to change it."

"That your old car out there in front of the house with a flat tire?" Kade asked irritably.

"Yes," she admitted.

"I'll help you. Let's go." He grabbed her hand abruptly and strode out of the house, making her jog behind to keep up.

Asha sighed, knowing she was about to have her second crucial confrontation of the day, except this one wouldn't just wound her feelings—it would rupture her heart.

Chapter 14

Asha stopped abruptly, slamming into Kade's massive body as they arrived outside, the door closing quietly behind them. He'd halted unexpectedly right outside the door and crowded her against the wall right next to the door. He leaned into her, his chest heaving, one hand against the wall on both sides of her body, effectively trapping her.

"I swore I wasn't going to do this," he said in a husky, desperate voice, his eyes boring into hers, his forehead damp with sweat. "I swore I wasn't going to react when I saw you again. Why the hell should I care about a woman who doesn't give a shit about me?" One of his hands fisted and slammed against the wooden exterior of Max's house in a gesture of frustration.

Asha looked up at him, her heart clenching at the exhaustion and torment showing on his face. "I do care, Kade."

"Bullshit. You left. You didn't even say good-bye. You never called to let me know how you were doing or if you were okay. I wasn't even a blip on your radar," he spat out resentfully.

"There hasn't been a day, or even an hour, that I haven't thought about you." *Or a moment, for that matter.* Kade haunted her constantly. "I missed you."

Time stopped as Kade searched her face, as though trying to figure out exactly what she was thinking. "I can tell," he answered sarcastically. "You tried so hard to stay in touch—"

"I couldn't, okay!" she shouted at him. "Everything about you confuses me. You waltz into my life with all your kindness and sexy male hotness." She took a breath and waved a hand at Kade, the aforementioned hot male. "Then you overwhelm me with your thoughtfulness, ply me with food, and then make me climax until I think I'm losing my mind." She jammed a finger into his chest. "You made me into nothing but female hormones that were always willing to hop onto your...your... testosterone," she finished awkwardly. "I couldn't think about anything but you, and I still can't. So don't tell me I didn't miss you. I've lost count of how many times an hour I dial half your number and then hang up the phone."

"Maybe you should have dialed the other half of the number," Kade said hoarsely.

Asha rolled her eyes, still on a roll. "I couldn't. I knew if I did, I'd want to see you even if you didn't want to see me." She pushed on his chest, trying to break away from his confinement.

"Then see me, Asha. Please. Because I want to see you," Kade argued persistently, not letting her break away.

"And then what? We'd just end up having incredible sex," she accused him anxiously.

Kade's lips twitched as he looked down at her. "And that's a bad thing...um...why exactly?"

"Because I can't think when that happens. There has to be more than just good sex," she blurted out, still trying desperately to make Kade understand.

"It's never been just good sex," Kade retorted angrily. "It's good sex because there's more than that between us."

Asha shuddered as she remembered having relations with her ex-husband, and the lack of emotion, the way she detached herself from the act. She knew Kade was right. Problem was, she couldn't exactly blurt out how much she loved him, and her concern was how he felt about her. "Is it different for you? I mean...with us?"

"If you're asking if I've ever fucked and felt the way I do with you, the answer is no," he replied hotly. "You rock my world just as much as I rock yours. Difference is, I'm not afraid of it. Hell, I *want* to feel that way. It's exhilarating and exciting, and it makes me feel more alive than I've felt in a very long time...maybe ever. And I sure as hell don't want to walk away from it."

"Then maybe I'm just a coward." Asha broke Kade's gaze and lowered her head. "Maybe I just can't handle it."

"Bullshit. That was no coward who just basically told her foster parents to go to hell. It's taken a lot of courage to do some of the things you've done, and you get braver all the time. In fact, I think you're actually developing a temper." Kade reached down and tipped her chin up and grinned. "Did you really just accuse me of trying to sway you with sexy male hotness?"

"It's true," she told him stubbornly. "Not that you can probably help it, but it's distracting."

Kade nodded. "Good. I want to be a distraction for you because you drive me completely insane." He swooped down and kissed up the side of her neck, nuzzling her ear as he whispered, "Just your scent makes me hard, and all I have to do is hear your voice or see your face and I'm ruined. Let me see you, Asha. Let me show you how good being together can be. Running away isn't going to resolve this for either of us. It's not going away."

Asha shivered at the feel of his warm breath on the side of her face, his lips lightly caressing her skin. She knew he was right, and she'd either have to see this thing through with him or continue running away from it. And she didn't want to run away anymore, especially not from Kade. She wanted to run toward him, fling herself in his arms where everything in her world felt right, and continue to love him with every beat of her heart like she already did. Being with Kade made her feel alive, too, except he'd actually brought her to life for the first time, breathed life into her. "Yes," she whispered softly, wrapping her arms around his neck. "If you want to see me...then see me."

Kade cupped her face in his large hands as he answered with passionate conviction, "I already see you, sweetheart. I always have."

Asha sighed happily as his lips captured hers, opening her mouth to taste him. He tasted like coffee and pure sin, and she savored him. One long, lingering kiss turned into another, until he finally pulled her head against his chest and held her so tightly she almost squealed.

"Thank God," he growled fiercely, his hands stroking over her back. "I know what you've been through, and I know I pushed you too hard, but having you leave nearly killed me. I wanted to come after you, but I couldn't get past the fact that you didn't want me."

"I did want you," Asha murmured against his chest. "How could you come after me if you didn't know where I was?"

Kade pulled back, putting a possessive arm around her waist and walked her down Max's steps. "I knew exactly where you were."

Asha snorted. "Is there anyone who *doesn't* know where I live?"

Kade shot her a grin. "Not anyone who cares about you. And the people who do have some pretty scary influence and connections."

"I noticed," she grumbled softly. "My car—"

"Needs to be junked," Kade interrupted irritably. "The tires are shot and who knows what might be wrong with it mechanically. Couldn't you have bought something a little newer?"

"It wasn't in my budget. I'm saving. And there's nothing wrong with it. It just needs tires," Asha remarked defensively. "My neighbor checked it over. He said it looked good except for the tires."

"Was he looking at you or the car when he said it?" Kade grumbled. "Some kid?"

"Tate happens to be about your age. And he knows cars."

"He's a jackass," Kade muttered, leading Asha over to the motorcycle parked in the driveway. "I'll take you home and have new tires put on your car. And I'm having it checked over mechanically, even though your knowledgeable neighbor already said it's safe."

Asha took a breath to argue, but Kade held up a hand and cut her off. "Don't even start. You can give me this much. Let me know you're safe."

She let the breath out and smiled. Yeah…she could. He was trying to help her, and she accepted gracefully. Looking at the motorcycle, which looked like a high-tech vehicle, she admitted ruefully, "I've never ridden on one of these." And honestly, she'd never wanted to.

"Then you haven't really lived." He opened the saddlebag and pulled out a helmet as he grabbed his own from the seat.

"It looks...fancy. Is it fast?"

Kade pulled a leather jacket out of the saddlebag too, and closed the door. "This is a BMW touring bike. Not as fast as my racing bike, but fast enough," he answered with a boyish grin. "Here." He held up the jacket so she could slip her arms inside.

"It's over seventy degrees today," Asha argued, not really crazy about the idea of putting on a leather jacket while Kade was in a short-sleeved maroon t-shirt, jeans, and black biker boots. She was attired much the same, except she was wearing sneakers rather than boots.

"It's lightweight and it isn't for warmth. It's protection," he told her adamantly.

She sighed and put her arms into the jacket, letting it swallow her upper body. It obviously belonged to Kade. "It smells like you," she said dreamily, his scent surrounding her.

"Sweetheart, if I hear you say something like that in that *fuck-me* tone of voice again, I'll be compelled to make you come right here in Max's driveway," Kade threatened, his words a grunt of warning.

Asha's gut clenched in reaction, a pulse of electricity flowing from her belly to her pussy. Her panties dampened as she pulled the lining of the jacket to her face and inhaled, but she stayed silent.

"Woman, you're pushing my buttons," Kade cautioned in a low, vibrating voice as he rolled up the sleeves of the jacket and zipped it.

She was swimming in the coat, the material coming down to her thighs. It was way too warm, but she didn't complain. Asha reveled in the way that Kade was watching out for her, protecting her. "So what do I do?" she asked, slightly intimidated by the large motorcycle.

"Hold on," Kade told her jokingly, but went through the basics.

Once they were situated on the motorcycle, Asha wrapped her arms around Kade and scooted up against his back.

"Tighter," Kade ordered huskily. "And don't let go."

The helmets had Bluetooth, and Kade had already explained it, but the sound of his voice in her ear still startled her.

Once the bike was in motion, Kade didn't have to tell her to hold tight. She started with a death grip around him, but tried to relax and stay neutral in position like he'd asked her to do. Most of her fear fled as she experienced Kade's competence at riding. His motions were smooth and fluid, and he rode with a confidence of a man who had been riding for a very long time.

"You okay?" Kade asked quietly.

"Yeah," she breathed softly. "This is great. Can we go faster?" Asha trusted Kade, and the feeling of freedom she felt from riding in the open air was exhilarating.

She heard Kade chuckle. "No, we can't, my little speed demon. I'm doing the speed limit. I'm carrying precious cargo." He hesitated for a moment. "We can get on the freeway. I know a place where we can go faster safely."

"Yes," she agreed readily. "Go."

The speed on the freeway was heady, and Asha clung to Kade, enjoying the ride with unrestrained abandon.

"I'm getting off at this exit," he warned her after they had gotten out of the city, letting her know they were going to slow to a stop.

"Where are we?" she asked curiously.

"You'll see," he answered mysteriously.

After driving for about five minutes, they arrived at what looked like a large arena. Kade stopped at the gates and punched a code into a panel, waiting until the gates opened enough for them to slip through. They moved down a narrow passage that opened into a large, paved racetrack.

"Do you know who owns this?" she asked inquisitively, excitement in her voice.

"Yes. Quite well. He happens to be my brother. This is Travis's track. He races cars as a hobby. He's a damn good driver."

"He doesn't seem like the type to do anything like that," Asha answered, stunned that a conservative man like Travis had a dangerous hobby.

"One of his few quirks," Kade answered jokingly. "You ready? We aren't doing anything crazy. And if you get scared, just tell me." He pulled the bike onto the track and started to pick up speed.

"Okay," Asha agreed, her heart accelerating with the motorcycle. The track was composed of long straightaways where Kade accelerated quickly and had them flying down the linear areas, and slowing down for the corners. Nevertheless, Asha was laughing with pure delight as he sped down the track, making her feel like she was flying.

"Scared?" Kade asked as he slowed for a corner.

"No. I trust you," she admitted in a breathless voice.

"Fuck! You have no idea how long I've wanted to hear you say that," Kade answered in a graveled, serious voice.

"Can we go faster?" Asha begged.

"No. Neither one of us is dressed appropriately and this bike isn't meant for racing, my fearless woman. I think you need a trip to Disneyworld. You'd love it," Kade remarked as he slowed, bringing the bike to a stop on the side of the track.

"I've never been to any amusement park," Asha confirmed, trying to finger comb her hair below the helmet into some semblance of order.

"Why am I *not* surprised," Kade grumbled unhappily.

Asha got off first, Kade steadying the bike as she dismounted. He removed his helmet and then removed hers, stowing all the gear, including his leather jacket, in the saddlebags. "We can grab something to drink. Travis keeps his fridge stocked here."

"Kade?"

He took her hand and guided her toward what appeared to be garages. "Yeah?"

"Thank you for this. That was wonderful," she told him genuinely. "It was one of the best things I've ever done. One of the few things."

"Do I want to know about the others?" Kade asked, stopping at the door of the building.

"I can only think of one thing that felt more incredible." Asha grinned at him. "And I experienced that with you, too."

"That so?" he asked dangerously, pinning her against the door with his body.

Asha wrapped her arms around his neck, desperately needing to feel Kade skin-to-skin with her. "Yes." She looked up into his smoldering blue eyes and her heart skittered. He looked tense, the dark circles under his eyes more pronounced, and she wanted to sooth him, comfort him, make him lose himself in something other than the negative emotions he'd been experiencing for the last few months. In that moment, she hated what she'd had to do to get herself together. It was obvious that Kade cared. He might not love her, but he definitely stressed over her, worried about her. And she'd caused him pain.

"I'm so sorry I hurt you," she told him gently, smoothing the circles under his eyes and the lines of tension on his face. "I didn't mean to." Her hand slid down his chest, over his ripped abs and finally stroked over his jeans, caressing the sizeable erection trying to burst through the seams of the denim. "You're so hard."

"Fuck!" Kade captured her roaming hand in his own and went into the garage, tugging her behind him. "I need that drink to cool off. Don't start something I can't finish," he rumbled in an ominous tone.

They moved past several vehicles and ended up in an office that Asha assumed belonged to Travis. "I'll finish it," Asha told him quietly, feeling awkward to actually be sexually aggressive, but she wanted to be. She wanted to do things with Kade that she never wanted with any other man. Although she loved Kade's passionate alpha male sexuality, she longed to please him.

And she was beyond ready to spread her wings a little and try.

Chapter 15

Kade gulped hard, trying to swallow a lump in his throat that felt like it was the size of a small boulder. A look somewhere between desire and determination was radiating from her expression, and he knew she had something in mind, something that would probably turn him inside out and upside down...again.

Glancing around the office, he noted that there wasn't much here. There was a tattered couch, a desk and chair, and the fridge. The carpet looked anything but clean, smudges of grease from the garage dotting various areas of the floor. "I'm not taking you here," Kade told Asha roughly. "It's not clean."

Asha gave him a sultry smile and unbuttoned the top button of his jeans. "No problem. I plan to get...dirty."

"Asha, I—"

"Please let me," Asha said in a vulnerable voice. "I've never tried seducing a man before, and I've never tasted you, but I want to. I was never brave enough before."

Holy fuck! Kade nearly spent himself in his jeans as Asha slowly lowered his zipper and traced her fingers over his cock through the silken material of his boxers. Everything inside him wanted to strip her and bury himself inside her, but he didn't. This was a moment he wanted to savor, his little butterfly trusting him, trying to break away from her cocoon. Kade promised himself he wouldn't move, wouldn't spoil the moment. But Christ, it was going to be hard, and he wasn't sure how much *harder* it could get before he lost it. "Take control, Asha," he told her, nearly choking as her fingers inexpertly fumbled with the cock she'd just liberated from his jeans and boxers.

"I want to please you," she whispered, uncertainty making her voice tremble.

She pleased him just by existing, so having her hands on him was ecstasy. He reached down and covered her hand with his, showing her how to stroke him. "Kiss me," he demanded, unable to go another minute without somehow being inside her.

Taking her eyes off his cock, she lifted her head and placed her mouth to his, her tongue pushing boldly past his lips, searching for his tongue.

Don't take control. This is Asha's moment.

Kade told himself that over and over as Asha's tongue explored the recesses of his mouth, starting to enter and retreat, matching the pace with the pumps to his cock. Wrapping a hand around the back of his neck, she held him tightly, her fingers threaded through the hair at his nape.

When she finally pulled her mouth from his, she left him panting, his hand encouraging faster pumps to his cock. He couldn't take this for very long, not without being inside her.

Asha jerked her hand away suddenly, and he let her free with a superhuman effort. Really, he just wanted to jerk his cock until he came, release some of the tension that had built until he was nearing detonation.

She was jerking up his t-shirt. "Off," she ordered sternly, grasping and pulling the shirt upward.

Kade pulled it up and off, dropping it to the floor, and then wondered if he had made the right move in disposing of it. Asha's hands were everywhere, stroking over his tattoos and touching every inch of bare skin she could find. When her mouth started sucking on one of his nipples, he groaned, his entire body shuddering, needing her desperately. "Asha," he growled in a low warning. "I'm trying. But if you don't stop teasing me, I'm going to be inside you in about five seconds." There was only so much a guy could take, and experienced in seduction or not, Asha was the hottest woman on the planet to him. That roaming mouth had to stop.

"You're so beautiful, Kade. So handsome and perfectly made." Her voice was low and sensuous, but the awe in her tone was genuine. She stroked over his muscled biceps to his chest, her fingers touching every bulging, developed muscle until she finally reached his happy trail. As her finger descended down the hairline leading to his groin, Asha went to her knees, her mouth following her exploring finger.

No one had ever called him beautiful, or even handsome. Yeah… he worked out, and his body was okay except for his mangled leg, but Asha's words made him sweat bullets trying to control himself. His hands fisted to his side; he willed himself to let her explore, ignoring the bunched tendons in the back of his neck and the sensation of the blood pumping forcefully through his head—both of them!!

His knees nearly gave way as her sweet mouth touched his cock, licking the drop of pre-cum from the tip. "Sensitive there," he told her between clenched teeth. Holy hell, every area of his body felt hypersensitive at the moment.

Kade looked down at her just as she sucked his dick into her mouth like a lollipop, nearly making him come just from the sensation and visual. Unable to stop himself, he speared his fingers through her hair and guided her head in a bobbing motion, groaning with pleasure as her tongue slid along the underside of his engorged cock. "Baby, I won't last long." His words came out between pants, his breath sawing in and out of his lungs, his heart thundering so furiously that he felt like he was having a heart attack.

When she moaned around his cock…he completely lost it.

"I need to be inside you. Now." He pulled her up and tore open her jeans, yanking them down until they were tangled around one of her legs.

She looked at him, confused. "It wasn't good?" she asked hesitantly as he pulled her toward the couch.

"It was too good. But I'm not coming alone, sweetheart," he told her adamantly, needing to make Asha come as desperately as he needed to get off himself. He craved her sweet moans of pleasure as she found her release, and he needed to give that to her. Gone were the thoughts that this place was too dirty and crude. Their passion wasn't waiting for moonlight and silk sheets. The fiery storm of their desire was ready to break, and their surroundings no longer mattered. Kade just wanted her, any way he could get her. He was just that desperate.

"You tasted as good as you smell," she told him candidly, licking her lips as she looked up at him.

"Woman, you're dangerous." Kade looked at Asha's innocent expression and groaned. While her words weren't exactly meant to seduce, they did, and he knew he had reached his limits on control.

Placing her hands on the arm of the couch, he nudged a thigh between her legs, opening her to him. Her needy whimper was music to his ears as he slid his fingers between her thighs and circled her clit with his index finger. She was so hot, so wet and so ready for him. Mesmerized just from the feel of her velvety, moist heat, he slipped two fingers inside her, finding nothing but silken fire to greet him. "You feel so damn good, so tight and hot," Kade grunted, slowly pulling out and then in again, but deeper.

"Please," Asha mewled, her head lowering and her hair falling over her face in a silken curtain.

Kade's gut clenched in primal satisfaction. She wanted him inside her. Nothing else would do. It was the same for her as it was for him. But he loved to hear the proof of her need. Never had he been so desperate to get inside a woman. Not even close. Yet he drew it out to savor her pleasure, running his thumb over her clit, sensitizing her body, making her ready to come for him.

"Kade!" she screamed desperately. "Now."

Not.

Quite.

Yet.

He relished her demands, heartened by her level of trust and ability to give herself to him without restraint. She asked for what she wanted now, and she wanted *him*. And, by God, she'd get every single thing he could give her.

Moving his thumb harder, rougher over her clit made Asha push her hips back demandingly, seating her deeper onto his fingers buried inside her. She threw her head back, her hair still covering her face, and moaned, a long, strangled sound that signaled her impending orgasm.

Kade jerked his hand from between her legs and impaled her with his cock, thrusting as hard and as deep as he could possibly get, the joining of their bodies hot and carnal. "Come for me, Asha." He wouldn't last long, and he wanted her shaking with the power of her climax when he did.

"Then fuck me. Hard," she begged, her voice raspy.

Kade gave her what she wanted, thrusting in and out of her body, his groin slapping against her ass with every stroke, completely lost in her heat. The two of them came together like blue fire, the colorful flame threatening to incinerate them both.

He found release the moment Asha imploded, her body trembling and her core clenching his cock, milking him with every contraction. Kade bent over and wrapped his arms around Asha, pressing himself against her back, holding her while her body quivered, savoring the intimacy of being this close to someone. In that moment, there was only him and Asha, the two of them experiencing the same emotions, the same pleasure.

Moments later, he dropped onto the couch, taking her down with him. She was sprawled on top of him, but Kade figured it was better him than the couch, as he wasn't so sure how clean it was.

He wrapped his arms around her, holding her against his body, savoring the feel of her against him. The last few months without her had been agony, a pain he never wanted to feel again. His soul had been dark again, empty of the light that Asha had illuminated inside him, and he didn't want to ever be in that kind of hell again. He'd slept little, and functioned poorly, barely existing. Maybe he'd been like that before he met Asha, but he didn't remember it, hadn't really acknowledged it. Now, he knew the pain of losing her, and it wasn't happening again.

Asha was murmuring something in Telugu against his chest, so he didn't understand the words, but her voice was gentle and sweet.

"I didn't understand a word of that," he drawled quietly. "I hope it's all good."

She raised her head and smiled at him, making his heart hammer against the wall of his chest. "It's good," she agreed. "I missed you."

Kade had missed her, too, but he was afraid it would scare the shit out of her if he told her just how much. "I missed you, too." He kissed her forehead, and tucked her head against his chest. "Now I'll have someone who likes to ride with me in more ways than one," he said with a smirk on his face, but he was thrilled that Asha enjoyed being on his bike.

"Oh, yes," she said excitedly. "I love it. Can I learn how to ride one?"

Kade flinched, not happy about the thought of Asha on a motorcycle. "We'll see. We can start with something easy," he answered noncommittally. *Like a bicycle with training wheels!!*

Sighing happily, she said, "I'd like that."

Oh, hell. If it makes her happy, I'll try to teach her on something safe.

Who would have thought that the solemn Asha Paritala that he had met mere months ago would get a kick out of riding on his motorcycle?

"Does the butterfly get to fly free, yet?" Kade asked in a husky voice, hoping that she'd say yes. All he wanted was for her to be happy, free, loved, and unafraid of anything. He could tell that she was slowly starting to realize that she was…more. He was doubtful she realized yet what an incredible, sexy, and talented woman she was, but she would. He'd make sure she did.

She lifted her head from his chest and beamed at him. "Not yet. But I'm working on it."

Kade smiled back, a silly grin that went all the way to his heart.

Kade dropped Asha off at her apartment, making arrangements to bring her car to her the next day. As he walked her to her door, Asha contemplated asking him to stay. She knew the moment he left, she'd miss him. But she also knew she had some thinking to do, and plenty of growth left to accomplish before she could do much more than date Kade right now. Having sex with him was inevitable. The two of them couldn't be in the same room together without the need to be together.

Kade being Kade, he had stopped to feed her before taking her home. She wasn't exactly thin anymore, but judging by his reaction to some of her old habits, he was never going to stop trying to feed her. Although her body had already filled out, she'd eat. Kade had a protective instinct that wasn't going to go away, and some of the little things weren't worth arguing about with him.

"I've been thinking about opening a football camp. For kids with potential who can't afford to go to any real training camps. I have some buddies who have retired and are willing to do some work with me. Harrison would fund the program."

Asha looked up at Kade as they arrived at her apartment door, Kade's arm protectively around her waist. "I think that's wonderful," Asha answered, not the least bit surprised that Kade would fund a project for underprivileged kids. "Do you like working with kids?"

Kade shrugged. "I've done a little bit of work with camps in the past, but just guest visits. Nothing of my own. It was fun. And there are a lot of kids out there who can't afford the extras."

"And you miss football," Asha added, knowing Kade missed being involved in the sport. "You have a lot to give, Kade. So much you could teach them. I think it's a fantastic idea."

"I'm not sure how much they want to learn from a guy who can't even really run well anymore," Kade replied in a self-deprecating manner.

Asha turned as she reached her door, gaping at him. She grasped a handful of his t-shirt to bring him closer, and stared up into his eyes.

He actually means that. He thinks he's less now than he was before because of his accident.

"Do you really think those kids would care? To be taught by the great Kade Harrison would have any young boy who loves football incredibly excited. And you don't need to be able to run." Asha sighed, loosening her grip on his shirt, but keeping eye contact. "We had five kids beg for your autograph when we went to eat. You're recognized by every kid aspiring to play football. You can be a role model for them. Football is more than just physical ability and you know it. It's up here, too." She took her free hand and tapped a finger to her temple. "You could teach them that, Kade, and nobody can do it as well as you."

Kade put both his arms snugly around her waist as his lips began to twitch. "You don't like football. How do you know?"

"I have a small confession to make," she told him, wrapping her arms around his neck. "I watched almost every one of your games for the last two seasons that you were playing. When you went to the office, I watched and learned from the recorded games at your house. You were incredible. I could almost see the wheels turning in your brain, your concentration and focus while you were playing. While a lot of the other guys were out there letting the testosterone fly, you were plotting, planning. I don't think I ever saw you lose your temper."

He grinned down at her, visibly pleased. "I couldn't afford to lose my grip. Too much riding on me staying focused. But trust me, I have no lack of testosterone. I just couldn't let it loose on the field. You really watched my games?"

"Believe me, I already know you have more than your fair share of male hormones, but you were in control. I was mesmerized," Asha admitted. "And I learned a lot. There's a lot of strategy in the game, and you're a master at it. You still have all of that information, Kade. And I'm willing to bet you can still hit your target with your throwing arm. So please stop beating yourself up because of your leg. You have so much knowledge you could share with young players."

"Damn right I can hit my target," Kade told her gruffly, but he was still smiling. "I was a little hesitant because of my leg, but I want to do it."

"Then do it. You're still the great Kade Harrison. And I'll bet your butt still looks amazing in those tight pants," she told him teasingly. Really, she probably could bounce a quarter off his tight ass, and she couldn't help but admire it every time she caught a glimpse of him from behind. Kade was still poetry in motion when he moved, even with an injured leg.

Kade laughed, a booming sound that echoed in the hallway. "I don't plan on wearing the pants. I'll be there to teach."

"Well...damn," Asha said, disappointed. "And here I was going to offer to teach some yoga for you at the camp if I could see that butt in a pair of those pants," she teased.

"I've never seen you do yoga. I'll wear the football pants if I can see you in a pair of those yoga pants," Kade said hopefully.

Asha lifted a brow. "I don't even own a pair of them."

"I'll get you some in every color," Kade replied eagerly.

She swatted him on the arm playfully. "My neighbors were Indian and practiced both yoga and meditation. I learned from a very early age from them. I haven't done it for a while, but like you, I still have the knowledge here." She put a finger to her forehead.

"Believe it or not, I think yoga is incredibly beneficial for a football player. I did some yoga pre-season and during the off-season. It helped me maintain my range of motion and flexibility," Kade told her with a wink. "I'd still love to watch you do it."

"For your information, I usually do it when I'm alone and in my underwear or naked," she informed him innocently.

"Scratch the yoga pants. I'll go for *that* in a private viewing," he told her with an evil grin. "And I'll take you up on the offer to teach basic yoga to the kids, but I'm getting you a baggy pair of sweats for that. I don't want my fellow players who are helping out to be checking out your ass. Football players can be horny bastards."

Asha rolled her eyes at him, amused that he seemed to think that every man would look at her with lust in his eyes like he did. Honestly, no other man looked at her the way Kade did. "You'll be a great teacher," she told him truthfully, knowing that he'd also make a great father. He was a protective alpha male, but he also had such patience and kindness.

"Thanks," Kade replied, lowering his forehead to hers. "So much confidence in my abilities?"

"Yes," she answered quickly and adamantly. Really, she didn't think there was anything Kade couldn't do if he wanted to do it. He had a stubborn tenacity that would always make him succeed.

"Have I told you today how amazing I think you are?" Kade asked her huskily.

Asha's heart skipped a beat. His low baritone was sincere, and he obviously did think she was exceptional, for some unknown reason. Somehow, it made Asha feel lighter, more carefree. "Nope. You haven't."

"Then let me tell you now. Asha...you're an incredible woman, *my* incredible woman." He leaned down and kissed her then, a kiss that was slow and languorous, making her feel valued and treasured. It was sensual, but it was an embrace that wasn't meant to arouse. It was a sharing of emotions, a kiss of communication and intimacy.

It left Asha smiling, her feet still not on the ground for a very long time after she opened her apartment door and disappeared inside alone.

Chapter 16

"It looks incredible," Tate Colter told Asha as he stared at the finished wall in his apartment. "It looks even better than I thought it would. I wish..." He trailed off, his comment unfinished.

Asha looked at Tate curiously, wondering what he was going to say. She'd finished his wall completely today, putting the finishing touches into the scene. "You wish what?"

Tate shook his head. "Nothing. I forgot what I was going to say."

Asha knew he was lying, but she didn't push. She and Tate had become pretty good friends in a short period of time, but she wasn't comfortable enough to pry. "I enjoyed doing it." She tilted her head, examining the old fire engine and other equipment she'd put in the painting. "How did you become interested in antique fire equipment?" she asked curiously.

"I was a volunteer firefighter for a while in Colorado. I got interested in some of the old fire equipment," Tate answered smoothly, turning his back to her and moving into the kitchen. "You want to stay for dinner?"

Tate had gotten his cast removed and Asha could appreciate the rock-hard ass and Tate's solid, muscular build. He was incredibly handsome, and she could admire him in an aesthetic sort of way, with hair almost lighter than Kade's and gray eyes that could almost appear to be looking into one's soul. But as gorgeous as he was, Tate did absolutely nothing for her. It was as if her body only reacted and came to life for one man. "Can't. I have a dinner date. Kade's taking me to a fondue place for dinner tonight."

"Sissy food," Tate called back in a teasing voice. "I was willing to make steaks."

"It was my choice," Asha told Tate indignantly. "I heard about it from one of the women in my art class, and I wanted to try it."

She'd just started her classes this week, and they were pretty basic, but she enjoyed every moment of them. She could finally put terms to her techniques and the teacher was an incredible artist. Asha knew she could eventually learn plenty of new things from her, and she was eager to absorb knowledge.

Kade had spoiled her rotten from the moment she'd seen him again during that horrible confrontation with her foster parents three weeks ago. They'd been to Disneyworld, and she'd squealed with delight through every ride. In fact, he'd probably taken her to every tourist attraction in Florida, but he always seemed to come up with something new every time she saw him. Usually, there wasn't a day that passed without her seeing him. And they texted like teenagers, sending flirty and seductive messages back and forth like two people completely...in love.

Asha sighed and picked up her purse, ready to go back to her own apartment and get ready for Kade to take her to dinner.

"You going out with that guy who wears the atrocious shirts?" Tate asked as he walked back into the living room. "I saw him coming out of the elevator yesterday. Gotta be something wrong with a guy who dresses like that."

"I happen to love his shirts," Asha answered defensively and honestly. "They're colorful, bright, and gorgeous." *Just like him!*

"They're nasty," Tate grumbled, shaking his head.

Asha walked to the door, but turned around and looked at Tate again. "You like football. You don't recognize him?"

"Yeah. Kade Harrison," Tate answered immediately. "He was a hell of a quarterback, but he needs to work on his personal sense of style."

Asha knew Tate was ribbing her. He wasn't the snobby type, and he wasn't exactly a fancy dresser. "I think he looks very handsome. Yesterday was his hot chili pepper shirt. And he definitely looked...hot."

Tate snorted as she opened the door. "He needs work."

Asha looked back at him and told him assuredly, "He needs nothing. He's perfect just the way he is."

"In love with him, are you?" Tate asked as he joined Asha at the door. "Only a woman in love could think that about a man in bad shirts."

Enjoying the bantering with Tate, she answered haughtily, "At least Kade knows how to treat a woman, unlike some men I know." She raised a brow at him, referring to the brunette who left his apartment every day smiling while Tate insisted it was a casual thing. "I haven't seen her for a few weeks. Did you dump her?"

Tate shrugged uncomfortably. "We...broke up."

"Are you sad?" Asha asked curiously, feeling bad that she had given him a hard time.

"Nah. It was bound to happen. She got back together with her ex-husband. I told you it was nothing."

Asha looked at Tate, but he avoided eye contact with her.

"I'm sorry." And she was sorry. If the woman had dumped him, even if he wasn't all that attached to her, it probably hurt.

"Don't be," he said hurriedly. "Maybe I can give your star quarterback a run for his money. I'm unattached," he said jokingly.

"I'm not," she told him cheekily, knowing Tate wasn't really interested in her. Pulling her keys from her purse, she walked across the hall to her own apartment.

"I don't see a ring. He doesn't have you, yet," Tate called from his doorway.

Asha unlocked her door and pushed it open. She paused for a moment before looking Tate straight in the eye from the door of her apartment. "He has my heart," she stated simply, closing the door of her apartment with a small smile.

Glancing at the clock on the wall of her apartment, Asha knew she'd have to hurry to get ready for her dinner date with Kade. A rush of adrenaline and excitement flooded her body as she moved quickly to the bathroom to shower. Not that Kade would mind if she was late. He'd wait patiently, understanding that she'd had to finish a job today, acting like he was perfectly content just to be in the same space with her. Although he was a billionaire who headed one of the most prestigious companies in the world, he never treated her obligations like they were any less important than his. It was one of the many things that Asha loved about Kade. He made her feel like she was important, that what she valued was also significant to him. Most of the time, he put her needs before his own, and it was starting to get less and less confusing for her. Kade cared for her, and he protected those he cared about and treated them with consideration. At one time, that had been foreign to her, but she was getting used to being treated as a woman of value by not only Kade, but by others such as Maddie, Max, Devi, and people she had met who were slowly becoming friends. It was still amazing to Asha that as people had started to value her, she'd started to develop her own self-worth.

Asha sighed as she stepped from the shower and wrapped herself in a towel. Padding over to the closet, she rifled through her clothing, picking a lightweight dress from the collection that Maddie and Mia had purchased for her when she'd first arrived in Florida. After countless discussions about the clothes, Maddie had shown up at her door a week ago with a very large moving man to bring all the clothing to her room to be hung in her closet. Maddie had given Asha a *don't-screw-with-the-pregnant-woman* glare, and Asha hadn't argued. Her sister might be sweet, but she had a stubborn streak when she wanted something. And she had wanted Asha to accept her gift. Maddie's brilliant, happy smile when Asha had nodded her agreement had been worth swallowing her pride. She'd made Maddie genuinely happy by finally accepting the clothes. It was almost symbolic, as if Asha had finally accepted her as a sister. Had Asha realized that it had meant so much to Maddie, she would have taken them before. But she hadn't been perceptive enough then to read her sister. Now...she was beginning to understand Maddie, see her through the loving eyes of a sister. The last thing Maddie needed right now was conflict. She was having twins, and the stress of the pregnancy was enough. Asha wanted to be there for Maddie, too.

The same day that Maddie brought the clothes, she just found out she and Sam were having a boy and girl. Asha's heart had first clenched with joy for Maddie when her sister had happily delivered her news, and then for herself because she was going to be an aunt to a new niece and nephew in just a few months. She and Maddie had cried tears of joy together, and it had been at that profound moment that it really hit Asha that she really had family. It no longer mattered what Max and Maddie had or how successful they had become. They were all irrevocably connected, and status meant very little next to the affection she had for both of them. Money or no money, Asha couldn't have asked for better siblings, and she was grateful every single day for them. She talked to Maddie and Max most days now, and spent as much time with them as she could, getting to know them both.

Lunch with Maddie, Mia, and Kara had become a weekly event, and Asha was still just a little in awe of all three women and their relationships with three very alpha, powerful men. The women were all independent and strong, but they adored their possessive, protective, and bossy husbands because those men wanted them safe and happy. It wasn't about control for any of the women's husbands. It was all about loving so strongly that they couldn't help themselves.

"Really, it all comes down to love," Asha whispered to herself as she smoothed the dress over her new curves. Didn't she love Kade's overprotectiveness and alpha possessiveness? And didn't she know it was because he cared? Maddie said there was a big difference between "alpha" and "asshole" and Asha completely understood exactly what her sister was saying. The distinguishing factor was all about what motivated their behavior.

Looking at herself in the mirror, Asha applied some light make-up and began French braiding her hair. She smiled, knowing Kade would just unbraid it later. It had become almost a sexy ritual for them, and she shivered as she braided, knowing it would be Kade's fingers that would set the strands of hair free again.

Finished, she took a final glance at herself, noting the way the jade green silk dress caressed her curves. It was cut just above the knee, but a small side slit revealed enticing glimpses of her thighs when she moved. Kade would like it, but he'd grumble about the amount of leg she was showing, and glare at any man who looked. Smiling, she snatched up her strappy sandals and her purse, glad she didn't need stockings. Even though she was of mixed heritage, her complexion was dusky enough that wearing stockings was completely unnecessary.

Asha forced herself to ignore the voice of her foster mother in her head that told her to cover her body, that she was exposing too much skin. Raised to be incredibly modest, the dress was a little out of her comfort zone for going out in public. Shaking herself mentally, she reminded herself that it was actually pretty tame by American standards. Still, it was hard to shake her upbringing and the idea that dressing to expose skin made her a "bad girl" who was asking to be assaulted or abused by a man.

Adding a pair of dangling, beaded earrings and her gold bangles, Asha declared herself ready and headed out to the living room.

Seven o'clock.

Kade should arrive any time. He'd said seven thirty, but he was usually early.

Asha was about to bend down to strap on her sandals when a beefy arm wrapped around her neck, startling a panicked scream from her mouth.

"Shut up. You are dressed like a whore, Asha," a heavily accented male voice said vehemently in her ear.

Asha had known it was Ravi from the moment the strong, male arm had wrapped around her neck. She'd been in the very same position many times before, and she recognized his painful grip and the sweaty scent of his large body. "H-how did you get in here? How did you find me?"

His hold tightened and Asha was starting to see stars flitting across her vision. "You're my wife, a married Indian woman. Yet you go around with another man. An American," Ravi answered angrily in Telugu. "You weren't difficult to find. All I had to do was follow him to you. You disgrace me."

Before, she would have trembled with fear, waiting for the first blow, which would be followed by many more, leaving her damaged and weeping on the floor. Now, anger began to swell up inside her, a rage for the man who had nearly broken her. "I'm no longer your wife. And I'm an American woman with Indian blood. Let go of me or I'll have you arrested."

Fight! Fight! Fight!

For the first time, Asha felt the instinct to fight for her life, for her sanity. At one time, all she had worried about was angering Ravi more, extending her beating. Now she wanted free, unable to ignore the feelings of hatred and fury that she had for the man holding her prisoner.

He laughed bitterly before announcing, "The police are already trying to arrest me. Your friends and family decided to poke their noses into my business, both personal and otherwise. I won't go to an American prison. I will die. But you will die with me, little wife. You've decided our fate." Ravi's voice was deranged and desperate, and his breath reeked of alcohol.

Asha's stomach dropped, wondering what Ravi was saying. Her family had pursued him? Had a warrant out for his arrest? Why? Questions flooded her brain, but her survival instinct was stronger. "I'm not your wife anymore. Let me go," Asha rasped desperately. She yanked at the arm pushing on her trachea, making it difficult to talk or breathe.

"You die with me," Ravi answered maniacally. "We married for life. You betrayed me."

Pulling her arm back, Asha thrust her elbow into his body with as much force as she could muster, hoping to hurt Ravi enough to loosen his grasp. She followed that action with a stomp of her foot on his instep, but she already knew she wouldn't do much damage without shoes.

"You dare to try to hit me?" Ravi howled, his arm lowering to capture her shoulders and arms in his grip.

Fight! Fight! Fight!

Asha gulped in breaths, grateful for the release of the death grip on her throat…until she felt the sharp edge of a knife nick the skin of her neck.

All the years of struggle, the years in poverty trying to obtain her freedom—all for nothing? This was how it was going to end? She was going to die at her ex-husband's hand after all?

First, reverting to old habits, she closed her eyes in silent resignation, waiting for the fatal cut.

But almost immediately, she decided her life and the people she had come to love were worth it to at least go down fighting. In a flash, she saw Kade, Max, Maddie, and all the other people who had helped her find value in herself.

She fought for them.

And she battled for her life.

Because she finally felt worthy.

She didn't deserve to die.

Unfortunately, she wasn't sure her resolve was going to be enough.

"What the fuck do you mean? He's gone? Where?" Kade barked at Travis as he drove, raising his voice in frustration as he talked to his brother on his phone connection from his car.

"We don't know," Travis answered gravely. "The police went to pick him up on a warrant and he'd disappeared. Nobody had seen him in days. Obviously he got wind of the fact that he was going to be arrested and fled. We removed the two women he'd raped and assaulted who were in his employ to get them some help. It probably tipped him off."

"Shit!" Kade slammed his hand on the steering wheel. "We need to find the bastard. He needs to be in jail."

"He could have flown back to India. We're looking for him. But he could be long gone," Travis answered unhappily.

"Asha and those women deserve to have justice done," Kade replied angrily. "The world would be a better place without him in it."

"You need to keep a cool head until we find him," Travis warned sternly. "Are you going to tell Asha?"

Kade gripped the steering wheel hard, his hatred for the man who had hurt Asha out of control. "What? That her ex-husband raped and assaulted two of his employees? Or that he's running around free after doing it?" He took a deep breath, trying to calm his desire for violence. "Yeah. I won't lie to her. I'll tell her the truth. I know her and I know the fact that he hurt other women will haunt her, but she deserves to know."

"It won't change anything," Travis pointed out rationally.

"It won't," Kade agreed. "But I won't have secrets between us. And she'll probably have to become involved with the case, probably testify."

"The guy is warped. If he knows the police are after him, he probably knows the original investigation came from us," Travis said distractedly.

Kade's whole body went tense, his mind suddenly fixed on a nightmare scenario. "You think he'd go after Asha?" He could barely voice the possibility.

"Doubtful," Travis replied immediately. "He's on the run. But I think you should keep an eye on her until he's found."

"I'm almost there. I'm taking her home with me. She belongs with me," Kade said, putting his foot down on the accelerator of his Lamborghini to get him to Asha's apartment as fast as he could get there. Something about this whole situation didn't feel right, and some primitive instinct was gnawing at his gut to get to Asha.

"Kade, I know you care about this woman, but—"

"I don't just care about her, I fucking love her," Kade interrupted his brother furiously. "I love her so much that I can't think straight. I want to kill anyone who hurts her, and I can't stand the thought of her having one moment of unhappiness after all she's been through. I think about her all day long, and I dream about her at night. There's no hope on this one, Trav. She's it for me. She's my life now. I'm right there with Simon, Sam, and Max." It was a place he'd never dreamed he'd one day be, but he didn't regret it.

Travis sighed. "Shit," he mumbled irritably. "So I'm going to be the only survivor. The only sane guy in our group?"

"I'm not so sure sane is all that great," Kade replied. "It's lonely and dark. I'd rather be certifiable and have Asha in my life."

"Don't expect me to visit you in the psych ward after she dumps you. I haven't found a woman yet who's worth losing my common sense over," Travis drawled, his tone dark and broody.

Kade knew Travis was putting on a front, a mask for all the emotions that lay behind the cynicism. He gave Travis his usual answer. "You're an asshole."

"I know," Travis answered agreeably.

Kade turned a sharp corner, his mind focused on Asha. "I'm almost there. I'll call you later," Kade told Travis impatiently.

"Something's up. I can feel it. Be careful," Travis said soberly.

Kade didn't question Travis's intuition. They were twins, and sometimes they could sense each other's emotions. And, although Travis would never admit it, he had a rather eerie ability to read and feel future events. Only Travis knew if it was just incredible intuition, or if there was more to his ability. He refused to talk much about it.

"Later," Kade replied simply, clicking the button to end their communication as he pulled into the parking lot of Asha's apartment building, and jumped out of the car the moment he killed the engine.

The sound of sirens wailing, sounding like they were headed in his direction, made Kade's entire body tense as he jogged awkwardly toward the building, knowing he wasn't going to relax until he saw for himself that Asha was safe.

"Fuck! She's coming home with me tonight and she's staying forever," Kade whispered harshly to himself as he reached the elevator, pushing the *up* button impatiently.

Kade's patience was gone, and all he could think about was keeping Asha beside him where she belonged before he lost his mind.

His jaw set, his mind made up, the elevator door closed on Kade's stony, determined expression as he jammed the button for her floor, more than ready to throw Asha over his shoulder and take her home—whether she was ready or not.

Chapter 17

Asha put all of the rage from her oppressed years into her life-and-death battle with Ravi, but it wasn't enough. He had her on the floor, his pungent body odor nearly gagging her. Her ex-husband's temper had always been on a short leash, blaming the world for his problems and taking them all out on her. But something was different, the wild look in his eyes telling her his mind had completely snapped. It was obvious he hadn't showered in days, and his number-one priority was seeing her dead. At one time, she'd been afraid he would kill her by injury during a beating. Now, her death seemed to be his only purpose, his sole intent.

Her arms pinned to her side by Ravi's weight, Asha tried to buck him off her body, but she could barely budge him, his substantially heavier weight and level of strength hampering her efforts. He grasped her braid, using it as a weapon to keep her head still as he brought the knife to her vulnerable neck. Ranting in Telugu, he increased the pressure, the edge of the knife beginning to cut into her skin, but he didn't make the final slice.

Asha knew exactly what he wanted, and part of her wanted to beg for her life, but it wouldn't matter. Hadn't she begged his forgiveness in the past for perceived slights or wrongs that she hadn't committed? It hadn't saved her from a horrific beating, and begging wouldn't save her now. Staying mute, she met his dark, crazy eyes with a defiant stare, something she never would have done in the past. He was going to kill her, but she'd never apologize for who and what she was ever again.

She was Asha Paritala, daughter of a progressive Indian man who had helped Indian women become successful in America.

And the man above her was nothing but her murderer.

Prepared for a fatal blow, Asha was stunned as Ravi was lifted from her body faster than her eyes could follow, his body flung backward and onto the floor at her feet. Sitting up, she scrambled backward, watching in fascinated horror as Tate Colter easily stripped Ravi of the sharp knife, and left him lying on her floor bleeding, with a single and incredibly powerful strike to the face. Flipping the older Indian man over, Tate put a knee in his back, keeping him immobile as he dialed the police on a cell phone he'd pulled from his pocket.

"H-how d-did you know?" Asha asked Tate as he replaced the phone in his pocket and looked at her, his eyes running over her body clinically, as though he were looking for injuries.

"Travis texted me," he answered vaguely.

"Travis?" Asha tried to wrap her mind around the fact that Tate and Travis knew each other, but her whole body was trembling in reaction to her close call with death. "Are you a cop?"

"Friend. And ex-military Special Forces," Tate answered shortly. "You okay?" His voice became gentler and more concerned. "Your neck is bleeding."

"Yeah. I think so," she replied, knowing she was lucky to still be breathing. Considering the alternative, she *was* all right. She placed her hand to her neck, and it came away smeared with blood. "Just a scratch."

Tate nodded toward the bathroom. "You better clean it up before—"

"What the fuck happened?" Kade's roar reverberated through the room.

"—Kade gets here," Tate finished solemnly.

Asha turned and looked up at Kade, her heart still hammering from the stress of her near-death experience and her body trembling with reaction. Wrapping her arms around herself, she opened her mouth to answer, but Kade pulled her to her feet and started examining her cut before she could get any words out.

"The bastard cut you." Enraged, Kade tipped her head back gently, looking at the cut and then back at the man who Tate had restrained. "I don't suppose he's dead?" Kade asked Tate dangerously.

"Naw. I just coldcocked him. Police are on the way." Tate shot Kade a dubious glance. "She needs that cut cleaned."

"Bathroom's that way. I think you should take her. You know first aid better than I do," Kade said, his voice alarmingly low and guttural.

"I'm not leaving you alone with him. I promised Travis I wouldn't. I understand your anger, Kade, but he'll pay for what he's done," Tate answered, applying more weight to Ravi's back as he woke, babbling in angry Telugu.

Hearing the voice of her ex-husband again had Asha shaking with reaction. "Take me out of here, Kade. Please." Her whole world was tilting, confusion and fear getting the better of her at the moment.

"Take her. She needs you. Don't let your anger override everything else. It will ruin you. Taking a life, good or bad, changes a man," Tate told Kade harshly, his smoky gray eyes slightly haunted. "Make Asha your priority right now."

Kade scooped Asha up from the couch and wrapped her in his embrace. "She's always going to be my priority," Kade said hoarsely.

Tate nodded once in understanding, watching Kade as he picked up Asha to take her shivering form to the bathroom. Kade moved around the sofa, looking down at the man on the floor under Tate's knee with undisguised hatred. He stepped over his body with one foot, the other landing on the man's outstretched hand, Kade's heavily booted foot putting all of his weight down and grinding hard as Ravi screamed with pain. It was more than enough force and weight to crush several bones and break a few fingers.

"That's for Asha and the other women you raped, you sick bastard," Kade growled, moving forward with Asha still in his arms.

Tate smirked.

The police stormed the apartment with Ravi still screaming in pain.

His attention all on Asha, Kade never looked back.

Later that night, Asha sat in the middle of Kade's bed, devouring a sandwich and watching him pace the bedroom floor. He'd been ranting for hours, and he didn't look like he was the least bit wound down. After he'd brought her back to his house, taken care of her, made sure she had a tray of food and was safe and sound, he'd started rattling off a list of things he was going to do to keep her safe.

"I know you want to heal and be independent, but you can do those things right here with me. I want you under my protection," Kade continued his reasoning gruffly.

Asha watched him with a lustful eye as she nibbled at her sandwich. Wearing only a pair of pajama bottoms, he looked incredibly hot and one hundred percent stubborn, ornery male. "I'd rather be under you personally," Asha whispered longingly under her breath. She was wearing the top of his pajamas, and she could smell his tantalizing scent all over the garment.

"Did you say something?" Kade asked impatiently, turning around and pinning her with a sharp glance.

Asha waved her hand. "No, no. Go on." She covered her mouth with her hand, hiding a smile. She had gotten over her post near-death shock hours ago, and there was no place she felt safer than here in Kade's bedroom with him stalking around her like a pissed-off big cat.

She realized his tirade wasn't directed at her. It was directed at himself on her behalf. She needed to stop him soon, calm him down and make him realize that none of this was his fault. But watching his possessive, obsessive behavior toward her was just a little intoxicating.

When he stopped speaking to take a breath, she asked curiously, "So Tate Colter is another rich guy? A friend of yours?" They'd been to the police station to give a statement, and Tate had been there, but Asha hadn't really been able to talk to him for long. She was still reeling from the truth of what her husband had done to his two female employees and just how vile he truly was.

"Travis's buddy. I know him through Travis, but he's been friends with Travis since college."

"And he was your spy?" Asha asked innocently.

"It wasn't like that," Kade answered irritably. "Colter wanted to get out of Colorado until his leg healed. The winters are brutal and he was in a cast, on crutches. Travis found him a place."

"And that just happened to be across the hall from me? In the same apartment building? Why couldn't he stay with Travis? Or at least get a nicer place if he's that rich?" Asha hesitated for a moment before adding, "And how did he meet some woman in such a short length of time?"

Kade grimaced. "The woman was his sister. She's happily engaged, but she wanted to see Tate and make sure he was feeling all right after the accident. Yeah. Okay. We sort of thought it would be nice to have Tate there to watch out for you. You took off without contacting anyone. You obviously didn't want me or anyone else you knew around. Tate volunteered and we set up the apartment for him. Yeah...he's filthy rich, but he's lived everywhere. What he told you about being Special Forces was true. "

"I thought he was my friend," Asha said wistfully, disappointed that Tate had only hung around with her because of Travis and Kade.

"He is your friend. Believe me...if Colter didn't like you, he'd watch out for you, but he wouldn't give you the time of day. Tate's pretty raw. Just like Travis." Stopping in the middle of the room, Kade eyed her speculatively. "You like him?"

Asha shrugged. "Yeah. I do like him, even though he was only sent on a spying mission by you and Travis."

"He wasn't a damn spy. He was just there to help if you needed him. You were alone," Kade grumbled. "But I still want to kick his ass for approving that car." After a slight hesitation, Kade asked, "How much do you like him?"

Asha looked up at him, startled. Kade's voice was radiating jealousy, and his jaw muscles were twitching. In spite of those facts, he looked vulnerable.

"I like him as a friend. He was nice to me. He joked around with me. I haven't ever really had that before with a friend." She sighed. "But he's not you and he never will be." Asha slid off the bed and went to stand in front of Kade, never breaking eye contact. "When I thought I was going to die, the only thing I really regretted is that I never told you how I felt about you. Maybe I shouldn't tell you now, but I don't ever want to feel that way again. I want you to know exactly how I feel with no regrets."

"Tell me," Kade said huskily.

"I love you," Asha said in a low whisper, barely able to get the words out over the lump in her throat. "I know you didn't ask for it and you probably don't want it, but it's there, and I'm tired of trying to bury it. You're the one I was longing for in that picture I drew of myself, the hunger that I thought would never be satisfied. I think I've longed for you my whole life. I just didn't know it."

"Tell me you really mean it," Kade demanded. "But I'm warning you, I'm never fucking letting you go if you do. Oh hell, I'm never letting you go, anyway. But I want you to tell me."

"I mean it. But I don't want you to feel obligated because—"

Her words were effectively stopped by his mouth seizing hers, his hands on both sides of her head to keep her still as he devoured her. His kiss was alternately carnal and adoring, demanding and giving, his tongue and lips owning her, yet also giving himself to her. He grasped her ass, picking her up, his lips never breaking contact.

Asha found herself on the bed, Kade having hastily removed her tray of food, making his way to his closet, and returning with several of his ties. He dropped the ties on the bed and began unbuttoning his pajama shirt, baring her breasts as he came to the last button. "You look sexy as hell in my shirt, but I need you naked," he rasped, his expression serious and eerily calm.

She watched him, confused, as he looped a tie around her wrist and secured it over her head, repeating it with the other wrist. Too shocked to react when he was binding her, she finally asked in a perplexed voice, "What are you doing?"

"Tying you to the bed," Kade remarked absently, testing the ties to make sure they were secure.

Asha knew she should be mortified, but the feeling of being naked and at Kade's mercy made her pussy flood with heat. His solid, muscular body leaned over her and slipped her panties down her legs sensually, letting them glide along her legs until he pulled them completely off.

Kade had barely said a word since she'd blurted out her feelings for him, and his silence was becoming uncomfortable to her psyche, but his actions were heating her body to dangerous temperatures. "I can see that. Are you going to tell me why?" she questioned nervously. She'd literally put her life in Kade's hands, but she'd never seen him quite like this.

"I told you. I'm never letting you go." He stroked errant strands of hair from her face, and nipped at the side of her neck, his mouth finally nuzzling against her ear. "I plan to pleasure you until you're out of your mind and agree to marry me. I figure that's the only way I'll get you to agree."

Asha trembled as his husky, low whisper vibrated against her ear, his voice a silky, low purr that reminded her of a cat.

"I can't marry you, Kade," she informed him sadly.

I'm barren. I can't marry him. It wouldn't be fair to him.

"Figured you'd say that. So I guess it's my job to change your mind. You'll eventually understand that all I need is you, sweetheart. Because I love you, too. More than anything or anyone on this planet. And you're going to be mine," he warned dangerously. "So after I taste you until you're screaming my name, and fuck you into the most incredible climax you've ever had, maybe you'll agree. If not, I'll try again."

Tears trickled down her cheeks, tears of pure joy that Kade loved her, too. "Kade," she moaned, pulling against the ties that were binding her. "These are your good ties." She noticed the feeling of silk against her palms.

"Baby, they are very good ties right now," Kade answered in a wicked voice. "I have a feeling every time I wear one of them from now on my cock will be hard all day. All I'll be able to think about is the way you look right now, spread out on my bed, mine to love and satisfy. And so fucking beautiful that I can't believe you really love me."

He was barely touching her, the tips of his fingers still stroking her hair, but his naughty words were driving her insane. She could imagine exactly how she looked…wanton, needy, and ready to be fucked. It was exactly how she felt, and her core clenched almost painfully. "Believe it. I love you." She repeated the words she'd said earlier. "But I won't marry you."

"Ah…you will, sweetheart," Kade answered confidently.

Asha gripped the ties as Kade began his assault on her senses, one finger tracing her pebbled nipples languorously. Being restrained was alternately frustrating and erotic. Asha longed to touch Kade's hot, muscular body, but the bindings set her free to just feel.

"I never want to be inside another woman again. Not after being inside you," Kade told her right before his tongue followed the trail of his finger, the heated warmth on her sensitive nipple making Asha lift her hips in need. Then he bit gently, sending waves of erotic pulsation straight to her pussy.

She was desperate to feel his cock fill her, pound inside her until she felt claimed. "Please," she pleaded, unable to tolerate Kade's teasing.

"Marry me?" Kade asked roughly, his hand moving down her stomach and between her thighs, parting her wet folds.

"No," she moaned, shifting her hips up, pleading for friction on her clit.

Kade didn't give her anything near what she wanted. He teased the tiny bundle of nerves lightly, barely flicking her clit with his finger, ramping up her desperation until she was whimpering. "More," she panted.

Kade parted her thighs wide, leaving her open and exposed. Grabbing a pillow, he stuffed it under her ass, making her even more vulnerable to him. Asha closed her eyes as she felt his warm breath caress her glistening flesh, quivering with anticipation.

All teasing ended as Kade buried his mouth into her pussy, groaning as his tongue, lips, and teeth consumed her like a starving man. Every stroke of his tongue was deadly serious, intent on making her come. The pleasure was so intense that Asha reflexively tried to close her legs, but Kade pushed them wider, feasting greedily on the cream he was creating with his erotic touch.

"Oh, God. Kade. I can't take this," Asha moaned, her head thrashing on the pillow, her hands tearing at the restraints.

"Take it, sweetheart," Kade rumbled against her flesh. "Come apart for me."

Kade's teeth clamped gently to her clit, flicking it over and over again with his tongue. He thrust two fingers into her channel, fucking her deep and hard, while his tongue created waves of pleasure that had her moaning and thrashing on the bed, so desperate to come that she was focused only on Kade.

Her climax hit her like a speeding freight train…fast, hard, and devastating. Her whole body shook as Kade kept rocking her body with his tongue and fingers, pulling every drop of pleasure he could from her.

Asha lay there panting after it was over, feeling raw, vulnerable, and completely loved. She watched as Kade climbed up her body like a dangerous animal—strong, powerful, and incredibly male. His expression was almost feral, and Asha felt an answering carnal need rising inside her. "Fuck me, Kade. I need to feel you." She needed to be joined to him in the most primal of ways, and the urge was soul deep.

"I love you, Asha," he groaned, his cock thrusting into her with one deep, long stroke.

"Ah…" She sighed, her body opening to him immediately, naturally. "I love you," she echoed, needing to tell him again and again. She'd had to stifle the emotion for so long that it was a relief to finally be able to share that part of herself with him.

With her ass already elevated, Kade had only to grasp her hips and thrust. He wasn't gentle or easy. He rode her with the ferocity of a man who was coming completely undone. "Fuck! You're so damn beautiful," he rasped as his cock pummeled into her. "So hot. So tight. So damn mine. Never another woman. You're all I want. You were always meant to be mine."

Asha's heart thundered in her ears, her body quaking as Kade spoke the passionate, possessive words that clenched at her heart.

Wrapping her legs around his waist, she savored his hard possession, feeling a sense of finally being exactly where she was supposed to be. "Harder," she demanded, wanting to surrender completely to him.

Kade buried his cock inside her in deep, forceful strokes, dominating her senses until she reached her peak with volatile intensity. "Kade. Kade. Kade." She chanted as her body convulsed around him, her core milking him, causing him to flood her with his hot release.

Releasing a strangled groan, Kade leaned forward and quickly released her wrists. "Shit. I marked you."

Asha's breath was sawing in and out of her lungs as she felt the circulation returned to her fingers. "Worth it," she gasped, knowing the only reason she had marks was because Kade had sent her over the edge of reason.

"Never," Kade growled, rolling to his back and pulling her half over him and half beside him. "I never want to leave a mark on you."

Asha looked up at the faint lines and smiled. "Call them love marks. I couldn't help myself," she told him breathlessly. "I needed something to hold on to."

"Next time you can hold onto me," Kade answered irritably, kissing the faint line on her wrist.

"I don't know…that was pretty hot." Asha sighed and snuggled up to Kade's body.

"I can't fuck you into submission," Kade answered, wrapping his arms around her body and pulling her skin-to-skin with him.

"You can. Anytime you want to," Asha answered eagerly.

Kade grinned down at her. "That good, huh?"

She nodded and smiled. "I changed my mind. My answer is yes. You can't fuck me into submission for any reason other than pleasure, but you made love to me until I saw sense. I realized that we do belong together. I think we've both seen enough heartache in our lives. I just want to be happy together. And I can still heal and find out who I am when I'm with you. You're actually part of who I am. One of the best parts."

"You mean it?" Kade asked gruffly. "Tell me you're going to marry me."

Asha leaned up and beamed at him. "I'm going to marry you," she answered obligingly.

Kade rolled her under him and held her wrists over her head. "Say it again," he commanded.

Asha glanced up at his face, so strong and stormy, yet with a hint of vulnerability in his eyes.

"I'm going to marry you," she said louder and with even more conviction.

"It was inevitable, you know," Kade replied in a more cocky tone.

"Was it?" Asha answered happily. Really, how could she not be ecstatic when a man like Kade loved her and wanted to marry her so desperately?

"Yep. I would have hounded you until you said yes. I never give up."

She smiled at him, her love shining from her eyes. Kade's tenacity was one of the things she loved about him, and she was pretty sure he would have done just that.

He lifted himself off her and slid out of bed, coming back with a velvet box. He sat naked on the side of the bed and flipped the lid open. "You deserve a real proposal with flowers, candlelight, and a romantic dinner. And I'll give you all of that. But for now, could you just say you'll marry me one more time?"

Asha gaped at the ring in the box, the gems nestled in the gold nearly blinding her.

"I looked at plain solitaires, but they weren't you. I know you like color, so I decided on this." Kade pulled the ring from the box and reached for her hand.

Asha's hand trembled as Kade pushed the ring over her finger. It was so incredible that she was speechless. The middle was a huge diamond, but the surrounding stones were a perfusion of color, each one a different hue. "I'm Indian. My love for color is in my genes," she replied with a tremulous voice. "It's beautiful."

"When did you get these?" Kade fingered the thin, gold bangles on her wrist.

Asha explained how she'd always wanted bangles but had never been allowed to wear any. "So it was my one indulgence," she explained, her finger still moving over her engagement ring in awe. "Bangles are important to an Indian woman."

"I'll get you a new one to add to your collection every week," Kade told her huskily. "You'll never want for anything again, Asha. I swear."

Asha looked up from her ring and her eyes met Kade's. How lucky could a woman possibly be? He was everything she'd ever wanted and more. She'd gone from a lonely victim of domestic violence to the fiancée of a man who would do anything not to hurt her. Kade *would* give her everything she wanted, but she saw everything she needed reflected in his gaze.

"I don't want for a thing anymore," she answered honestly.

Asha wrapped her arms around his neck and kissed him, proving to him without words that his love would always be more than enough.

Chapter 18

"I think what Devi was trying to make me understand is that what happened with Ravi went beyond culture," Asha told Maddie as they sat at Maddie's kitchen table talking one morning. It had been two weeks since Kade had asked her to marry him, and she still rubbed her ring every few minutes, unable to believe she was actually going to marry a man like Kade Harrison.

Asha took a sip of her chai latte, while Maddie drank lemonade. Maddie looked across at Asha, answering, "You do understand that, don't you? Your foster parents and Ravi both had issues that went deeper than culture. And Ravi had a drinking problem."

Asha paused as she absorbed what Maddie had just said, and then continued, nodding. "Kade's taking me to India. I want to learn more about my father's country firsthand so I can contribute to the foundation and help out there, too. I know that India has gender inequality and a very high rate of domestic violence and that there are laws to protect women, but they're rarely enforced. I think some women just accept it as their lot in life. That many years of brainwashing is going to be hard to overcome, but I know it can be done."

"It's because they don't know anything different," Maddie injected softly. "I see a little of the same mentality here in the United States, too, in domestic abuse issues. Too many women accept it because their self-esteem has been undermined and manipulated by the man or men in their life. Unfortunately, it's more the norm and more common in India than it is here in the US."

Asha's enthusiasm for her newfound cause was evident. "I think the younger generation is starting to move for gender equality, but there's still a long way to go. Devi does some work over there to help women fighting for equality and I want to be part of it. There are also some beautiful things I'd like to see in my father's country."

"I think your dad would be proud that you want to continue his legacy," Maddie said gently.

Asha nodded. "I think so, too. But it's not just for him. It's for me, too. I know what it's like to be held back and punished just because I was born female. I'm lucky enough to be free of that now. I'm still a work in progress when it comes to getting rid of my old baggage, but I'm working on it."

"And Kade?" Maddie prompted.

"Is so incredibly supportive that he makes me cry almost daily." Asha finished her sister's thought with a smile.

She fingered the two additional bangles that Kade had already added to her collection, intricate gold spirals with delicate designs, one of them bursting with a variety of color. Both were much more detailed than the ones she'd bought for herself, and incredibly beautiful. The only tiff they'd really had in the last few weeks had been his highhandedness over ditching her car and buying her a new one. It had ended with him apologizing for doing it without her knowledge, but he had stubbornly refused to return the new vehicle, asking her to drive it for him. Really, Kade made it so damn hard to refuse him when his reasoning all revolved around her safety.

Remembering something else she'd talked over with Dr. Miller, she asked Maddie, "I wanted to see if you could recommend a gynecologist. I'm late this month. I know it's just the stress of what's been happening, but I think I finally need to know exactly why I'm infertile. It's going to be vital to my healing process and acceptance."

Maddie's head jerked up and she pinned Asha with a calculating stare. "How late?"

Asha shrugged. "A week or two. It's no big deal."

"And you're emotional every day?" Maddie asked carefully. "Have you been sick or nauseated? Anything else out of the ordinary?"

"The smell of garlic seems to make me nauseous lately. I've had to stop cooking with it for now." She looked at her sister, the suspicious look on Maddie's face forcing her to add, "I'm not pregnant, Maddie. You know that's not possible. I only mentioned this because I think it's time for me to start dealing with reality instead of going through life with blinders. I need to know why I'm not fertile. Then I can move on. Kade accepts the fact that we'll never have natural children, and we'd both like to adopt someday." Asha's heart lightened at the thought. Kade was an extraordinary man, and she knew he really didn't care if he had children of his own. He truly believed that there were so many children in need of a good home that it didn't matter if his children were his blood or not.

Asha watched as her sister hurriedly rose to her feet as quickly as a woman who was carrying twin babies could get up. Popping to her feet, Asha grabbed Maddie's arm and helped her straighten. "What are you doing? You're supposed to be resting," Asha scolded, knowing Maddie was really starting to feel the effects of carrying twins.

"We need to see if you're pregnant," Maddie said excitedly, waddling out the kitchen door without another word.

Asha followed quietly behind her, putting a hand to her flat belly. No! She wasn't even going to consider the possibility. "Maddie...I shouldn't have mentioned it. I know I'm not."

Stopping in the downstairs bathroom, Maddie ignored her, rifling through her medicine cabinet until she had what she wanted. "Asha... no offense...but your ex-husband was the lowest scum on earth. Do you think he wouldn't lie?" She handed Asha the two pregnancy tests she had in her hand and waved at the toilet. "Pee. Now."

Asha grasped the pregnancy tests to her chest, her heart starting to gallop like a herd of wild horses. *What if...*

"I'm not pregnant," she told her sister again obstinately.

A small smile formed on Maddie's lips as she pushed Asha lightly into the bathroom. As she closed the door she said softly, "We'll see."

Alone in the bathroom, Asha pulled the first test out of the packaging. She was completely familiar with the tests. She'd used plenty of them early in her marriage, sad that she couldn't conceive, but secretly relieved every time they came back negative. But it would be different this time. Now, she'd give anything to see a positive result, even though the chances of that were pretty slim.

Gathering her courage, she tested twice.

Kade beat her home that evening. As Asha let herself into the house, she could smell something delicious in the air.

A man who cooks!

Kade's culinary talent might be limited, but he tried, and he'd even gotten some easy recipes from Sam.

Asha stood at the entry to the kitchen, silently watching her fiancé with awe. How had she ever gotten this lucky? Just a few years ago she'd been a battered wife, and now she was the cherished fiancée of the most wonderful man in the universe. With his wealth, looks, and personality, Kade could have had any woman of his choosing, yet he wanted *her*.

You are worthy. You are worthy. Asha chanted the mantra in her head, not completely sure she entirely believed it yet, but Dr. Miller said that acceptance would come with time. Right now, she just felt damned lucky.

Kade's head whipped around suddenly, as though he felt her presence. "Hey beautiful...I didn't hear you come in," he greeted her happily, his blue eyes reflecting nothing but love.

"I had a great view of your ass. I didn't want to ruin it," she told him jokingly as he swept her up in his usual hug, picking her up by the butt and kissing her as though he hadn't seen her in months. In reality, it had been just this morning.

"Get naked with me, and I'll be glad to let you look all you want," Kade whispered low and seductively against her ear.

Asha nearly let him take her away. Right now, the only thing she wanted was to be as close to Kade as she could get. "Dinner," she reminded him playfully, her arms around his neck, hugging him closely to her body. She could already feel the very hard proof that he could back up his promise quite easily.

"Okay. I do need to feed you first," he rumbled, letting her body slowly slide down his until her feet were back on the ground. "How was work?"

Asha rolled her eyes, wondering if Kade would ever get over wanting to feed her until she nearly popped. "I rescheduled the job for next week," she informed him carefully.

"So where were you, then? Found another guy already?" Kade's words were teasing, but his eyes were serious.

"I went to see Maddie this morning. And then I went to an appointment. It took awhile." Asha gnawed on her lip, not quite sure how to tell Kade what she needed to tell him.

"You okay?" The worry in his eyes increased.

"I'm fine." Asha put a palm to his stubble-covered cheek and smiled. "But I have something I need to talk to you about. Something important."

Kade took her hand from his cheek and kissed her palm. Flipping all the controls off on the stove, he grabbed himself a beer and sat a bottled water on the table. Pulling out her chair, he motioned for her to sit. She sat, and Kade flopped down in the chair on her right. "Talk," he said gruffly, all of his attention on her. "Whatever it is, we'll figure it out. As long as you aren't planning on telling me you won't marry me or you're leaving again, I can figure anything out."

"I'm pregnant." Asha blurted the words out before she could think about it. They had been bottled up inside her all day, and she needed the support of the person who mattered the most to her in the world. Seeing the incredulous look on his face, she babbled on. "I went to see Maddie this morning and I mentioned a couple of symptoms. She made me take a test. Two tests. Both positive. She made a few calls and got me in to a friend of hers, an OB doctor. She did a bunch of tests. My reproductive system appears to be fine and I'm pregnant." She buried her face in her hands. "Oh, God. I'm so sorry, Kade. I didn't know he'd lied. I didn't know I could get pregnant. I know you said you weren't sure you wanted—"

Kade snatched her out of her chair and had her in his lap so fast that it stopped her pathetic speech. Tears poured down her face, every emotion that had been tumbling around inside her suddenly bursting from her body at the same time.

Shock.

Surprise.

Anger.

Relief.

Regret.

Happiness.

And so many other feelings that Asha wasn't able to identify. "This should have been something we talked about, something we decided together," she told him regretfully.

Kade lifted the edge of his t-shirt and dabbed at her tears. "I think it took both of us to get you pregnant, Asha," he said gently. "Please don't cry. You don't want this baby?" He sounded unsure, a hint of hurt and confusion in his tone.

"I do want it. I want our child so much it hurts. But we had plans. And you said you weren't sure you wanted a child of your own. I should never have had sex with you until I knew the truth about why I wasn't able to conceive. Turns out that I can. Apparently Ravi lied."

"Not exactly a shocker," Kade rasped. "Bastard!" In a gentler tone, as he placed a hand on her belly gently, he continued, "I want this baby, too. I know what I said, and I could have easily adopted. But now that I know you're having our child, I'm ecstatic. I know she'll be as beautiful as her mother. I guess I'm a little in awe of the fact that we made a baby. Our baby."

Asha swiped at her tears. "Don't you want a boy?"

"Nope." He grinned at her, a smile that went all the way to his eyes, making them twinkle happily. "But I'd take a boy if that's what you give me. I'd be happy either way, sweetheart. He or she will be our child, and that's what will make the baby special, no matter what sex it turns out to be."

Asha digested that information and smiled back at Kade. "I'm used to men who want only boys." It was Indian culture to want a male child. Knowing Kade would love and nurture either one equally was still a bit of a culture shock. Then again, it shouldn't have been surprising. He was…Kade. "It will change our life a lot," she warned him.

"Plans are made to be changed. I want to get married right away. I wanted it soon, anyway. This seems like a convincing reason to do it tomorrow." He grinned at her wickedly.

Kade had been trying to talk her into a quick wedding since he'd proposed, and she'd wanted to wait awhile because Maddie would be due soon, and she wanted her sister at her wedding. "Maddie—"

"Maddie can come if we do just a few people at her and Sam's place. We'll put her feet up and she can be there," Kade said convincingly. "I already talked to her because I told her I couldn't wait. She offered."

Asha raised a brow at him. "She didn't tell me."

"I asked her not to tell. I was planning on convincing you tonight," Kade answered with a seductively evil grin.

"Are you tying me to the bed again?" Asha asked eagerly, blushing slightly. "You could always try to fuck me into submission again." She'd go for that.

"I'm not tying my pregnant fiancée to a bed," Kade answered in an adamant but awed voice.

"I can't believe I'm actually pregnant," Asha whispered, putting her hand over Kade's on her belly. "All those years when I thought I wasn't capable. This seems so surreal."

"What did the doctor say? Is everything okay? You should have called me. I would have gone with you." Kade sounded both irritated and worried.

"I didn't think about it. I thought it was all a mistake. I think I must have conceived in Travis's office at the racetrack. The doctor said everything is fine." She hesitated for a minute before she commented, "I suppose that means I won't be taking the riding course to get my motorcycle license right now."

"Hell, no!" Kade boomed. "You aren't even getting close to a bicycle right now."

Asha sighed. "I suppose this is going to make you into a tyrant." His protective nature was probably going to be nearly unbearable, but it was done with love. This was all new for both of them. "You'll get used to it," she told him casually. "We both will."

Kade tightened his arms around her body. "No I won't. Sam never has. The closer Maddie gets to her due date, the more frazzled he looks. I feel like I'm about to have a heart attack already, and the egg is barely fertilized, right? Damn. I need to borrow some of the books on childbirth from Sam. And we need to get stuff for a nursery. And a baby needs clothes and lots of other stuff. This house definitely isn't childproof. I need to work on that."

Asha took his head between her hands and kissed him, shutting down his frenzied words, and hopefully his overactive mind. She loved the way he cared enough to brood over her well-being and now the baby's, but when he got obsessive, she needed to find a way to calm him down. And kissing him seemed to be the only way to do it.

Kade took over the embrace almost immediately, kissing her with a passionate intensity that left her breathless. Both of them ended up panting, Asha resting her head on his shoulder. "You have time to do everything," Asha gasped. "And the last thing you need right now is to talk to Sam. He's a wreck. Maddie's having twins, so he'll probably tell you a bunch of horror stories about what could go wrong. Women have babies every day."

"It's different. *My* woman doesn't have *our* baby every day," Kade muttered.

"I love you. Take me to bed," she urged in her *fuck-me* voice that Kade had never been able to resist. "We can talk about everything later. Right now I just want to be close to you."

Her relief at the fact that Kade really wanted this baby as much as she did had her dizzy with happiness, and all she wanted was to be joined to the man she loved in the most elemental of ways.

"Food," Kade argued.

"You," Asha countered, sliding her hand down to the front of his jeans and gently grasping his hard cock through the denim. "I'm hungry for you."

Kade groaned. "I love you, too, and you're pushing me, woman."

"I know. I plan to push you right over the edge with pleasure," she answered naughtily. "All I need is you inside me right now."

Kade's big body shuddered, all of his defenses coming down as he looked into her eyes. "I want to give you anything and everything that will make you happy. That's all I want."

"Then you don't need to give me anything but your love," Asha told him honestly, her heart in her eyes as she stared back at him.

"Baby, you'll always have that," Kade told her confidently, standing up with her in his arms.

"Then I'll always be happy." Asha sighed as Kade strode toward the bedroom.

Kade didn't forget to feed her. But they ate later. Much later.

Epilogue

Two Months Later

"That looks good. Exactly what I would do," Kade told Asha encouragingly over her shoulder as she sat looking at her financial portfolio on her computer, the portfolio she was now building for their child.

She explained her rationale to him as she did her investing. Kade encouraged, and he pointed out pros and cons, but he let her figure things out on her own once she got the hang of thinking like an investor.

He'd calmed down considerably about the baby, but he never stopped worrying. Instead of his alpha male behavior irritating her, it actually comforted her. She was learning, especially from the women in her life, exactly how to handle Kade's occasional over-the-top behavior. Mostly, Asha felt loved, and that was a feeling she wouldn't trade for anything. Kade coddled her, cherished her, and downright spoiled her. In return, she tried to do the same for him. She supposed there was nothing she could really do to prove how much she loved him, but it didn't stop her from trying.

The last few months had been an adjustment period, but strangely, it hadn't been difficult. Considering they were married a few days after she'd discovered she was pregnant, Asha would have expected there to be some rough patches. There weren't. Not really. She and Kade just seemed to…fit, getting closer every day until she couldn't remember what her life had been like without him there, and she didn't want to remember. Kade was her best friend, her lover, and now her husband and the father of their unborn child. After her traumatic history, she felt like she was living a dream, a lovely dream that she hoped never ended.

"Coming from you, I'll take that as a compliment," Asha answered. "You're the smartest man I know." She signed out of her account and got up from the chair. "I guess it's time to get to Maddie's. I can't wait to hold the babies again."

Her sister had delivered slightly before her due date, but both babies were healthy and already driving their parents happily crazy because they weren't on the same feeding schedule. She and Kade had volunteered to give Sam and Maddie a night off so they could get out of the house. Truthfully, it was no sacrifice for either of them, as they were both completely enamored of their new niece and nephew.

"Do you really think we're going to be able to pull either one of them away from the babies?" Kade asked doubtfully.

"They're going," Asha answered stubbornly. "They both look worn-out. They need a break."

"Sam's gone from worrying about the birth to worrying about what college they're going to. That got me thinking—"

"Don't even start," Asha warned him, putting her arms around his neck. Kade and Sam were bad for each other when they started talking kids. When Simon got into the mix, it was even worse. Every one of them was more than ready to plan out the next eighteen years of their assorted children's lives for them before they could even talk.

"What?" Kade asked innocently, tightening his arms around Asha's waist. "We're just thinking about their futures."

"You can wait until they have some say in that future," Asha told him adamantly. "I can tell you from experience that it sucks to have your future planned out for you."

"I'd never do that," Kade said huskily. "You know I'd never force anything on our child."

Asha did know that. "I'm sorry. It's a touchy subject. I know you wouldn't." Kade was excited, and she didn't want to kill that excitement for him. "It's my own insecurities. It's not you. It's hormones. It seems like I'm either cranky, crying, hungry, or horny."

"But you're beautiful in any mood," Kade reminded her with a grin. "I prefer the horny mood, though."

A startled laugh escaped from Asha's mouth. It didn't matter what mood she was in; Kade could switch it from irritable to horny in a matter of seconds. She looked up at his beloved, handsome face and liquid eyes with a sigh. "My soul mate. I happen to prefer that mood myself," she told him with a grin.

"You are my soul mate, Asha. Do you remember when you asked me if I believed there was one person for each of us? I wasn't sure what I thought then, but I know now. If I get overbearing and annoying, just remember that I can't live without you anymore."

Asha nodded. "I know. I feel the same way." She lifted her foot onto the chair. "I redid my tattoo." Her henna tattoo had faded, and she'd replaced it with another image, using materials that she knew were safe for the baby.

Kade studied it for a moment before recognition dawned. "You changed it entirely. It's a phoenix rising, just like mine."

"I don't feel like a butterfly anymore," she admitted. "I feel like I've been reborn and I'm ready to start living for the first time. Because of you. A butterfly is too fragile. I feel stronger than that."

Kade tipped her chin up and kissed her. "You are strong. The strongest woman I've ever known." He fingered the delicate phoenix, tracing it with a finger. "There are very few people brave enough to escape the conditioning you went through and become their own person, no matter what the cost."

"I wasn't brave. I was just surviving," Asha told him, perplexed.

"Sometimes surviving is a whole lot braver than the alternative," Kade said gravely. "You're a miracle. My miracle."

Asha thought it was the other way around. "You saved me."

"You saved me, sweetheart," he contradicted.

"Maybe we should just say we saved each other," Asha answered, knowing the important role Kade had played at making her start to put the pieces of her shattered life back together again.

"The phoenix is perfect. You're right. The butterfly is too fragile," he mused. "And you're finally flying."

"Not yet. But I'm working on it."

"Anything I can do to make you fly higher?" Kade asked solemnly. He put her head on his shoulder and rocked her gently, his hold comforting and reassuring.

"Just love me," she murmured.

"Then you can be sure you'll always be soaring," he answered.

Asha pulled back to look once again at the phoenix rising, and she knew Kade was right. The butterfly that couldn't escape the cocoon was finally gone, replaced by a powerful mythological creature that would always be airborne. Right now, the phoenix was barely rising from the ashes, but with Kade's love, it would soon be flying high for the rest of her life.

How could it not? She had married a man who had loved her and wanted to marry her when he thought she was barren, but had easily become ecstatic about the idea of having an unplanned child of their own. Kade loved her unconditionally, and that continued to amaze her each and every day.

"I love you," she whispered as she gently kissed the strong line of his jaw. It was as if she couldn't tell him those words enough. They'd been bottled up inside her for so long that all she wanted to do was tell him how much he meant to her every day, several times a day.

Kade held her tighter and she lowered her foot to the floor to keep her balance.

"You know what it does to me to hear you say that," Kade growled, palming her ass.

She knew, but she told him anyway because she needed to say it and she loved the consequences.

Kade told her he loved her as he tore her clothes off and carried her to the bedroom.

They were a little late for their babysitting that night, but Sam and Maddie never said a word. Her sister took one look at Asha's swollen lips, tousled hair, and contented smile and winked at her as she and Sam went reluctantly out the door.

Asha winked back, smiling as she flipped the lock on the door behind them.

She entered the living room to find Kade holding both babies, one in each arm, all three of them asleep. Her heart turned over as she saw the protective way he held the babies, an arm curled around each tiny body.

It wasn't often that both of the twins slept at the same time, but Kade seemed to have the magic touch. Asha crept over to the couch and cuddled beside Kade, resting her head on his leg.

It was one of those moments when everything in her life was perfect.

She was with Kade, her nephew, and her niece.

Real family!

Asha knew she had finally found the place where she truly belonged. All her life, all she'd wanted was a real home. Finally, she realized that *home* wasn't just a place. It was a state of mind. And it was *him*. Life really *was* all about love, and as long as she was with Kade, she'd always be home.

~*The End*~

Please visit me at:
http://www.authorjsscott.com
http://www.facebook.com/authorjsscott

You can write to me at
jsscott_author@hotmail.com

You can also tweet
@AuthorJSScott

Look for Travis's book—coming soon!

Please sign up for my Newsletter for updates,
new releases and exclusive excerpts.

❦━━━━━━━━━━━━━❧

Books by J. S. Scott:

The Billionaire's Obsession Series:

The Billionaire's Obsession

Heart Of The Billionaire

The Billionaire's Salvation

The Billionaire's Angel
(part of a Duet – A Maine Christmas…Or Two)

The Billionaire's Game

27852383R00135

Made in the USA
Middletown, DE
22 December 2015